THE BARON AT LARGE

John Creasey
as Anthony Morton

The Baron at Large

WALKER AND COMPANY
New York

THE BARON AT LARGE

CHAPTER ONE

INVITATION

A man sat in a house at Barnes, and regarded with some annoyance a short, plump visitor, whose dark limpid eyes gazed back at him sleepily.

'You must not raise arguments, Mervin, I've told you that before. The Kallinov collection will be at *Beverley Towers* on the twenty-third, and we shall take it. Smith and Rogerson will operate, with help from inside.'

'Reliable help?' murmured Mervin.

'Of course! I am told, too, that the Baron will be present. It will be quite simple to encourage the police in thinking he is at the bottom of it.'

'Who *is* the Baron?' inquired Mervin, gently.

The other pursed his lips.

'I am not sure of his exact identity—few people are. But I am sure that he will be one of several guests at the house. The police, I understand, have their suspicions. At the first news of a robbery the Baron will immediately be suspect; it should not be difficult for us to strengthen that suspicion.'

'It could be done,' agreed Mervin.

'It *will* be done,' asserted the other firmly.

Mervin's eyes narrowed.

'I find it a little hard to believe that we can get our hands on a quarter of a million pounds'-worth of jewellery, with the Baron near by. Do Smith and Rogerson know he will be there?'

The other laughed harshly.

'Don't be a fool. Do you want to give them cold feet? They can learn about that afterwards.'

'If I were taking an active part in a burglary,' Mervin said, 'I should want to know a lot more. Who was helping me there, for instance.'

'They'll be told, on the night of the job.'

'You won't forget that I warned you of unforeseen difficulties, with the Baron about?'

'I won't need to remember,' snapped the other. 'The Kallinovs will disappear under the Baron's nose, and the police will take him. All right, I shan't want you any more.'

The man at the desk waited for the door to close on his visitor, then lifted the telephone.

John Mannering read the invitation with some amusement: Lord Sharron hoped that he would be able to visit *Beverley Towers* for the third weekend in January, and that he would bring the Gloria diamonds with him.

'For, as you know,' the letter went on, 'the whole Kallinov collection is now in England, and to collect each piece under the same roof will be an historic occasion.'

Three years before, such an invitation would have been tantamount to asking the Baron to raid the collection: but Sharron had no idea that the Baron and Mannering were the same man.

The one was a legend, the most successful and most feared jewel thief in England, the other, a man-about-town, member of one of the oldest families in the country. Only a few people had come to suspect that they were identical.

There had been a time when the Baron had robbed both for excitement and gain, but that was long past. The temptation, however, remained, and this was likely to strain it to the utmost, more especially as his interest in the Kallinov collection had always been keen.

Mannering, wondering what precautions Sharron would take against theft, could not repress a sharp regret that the Baron, as such, was dead.

He sat down and penned a note of acceptance, then set out to find whether Lorna Fauntley, the girl with whom he was in love, would be at Beverley. That her father, owner of three of the Kallinov pieces, would be there, was a certainty.

10 ✓

There was no real suspicion of malpractice about Mr. Matthew Mendleson, although he played the markets dangerously at times. Short, stocky, florid, his peculiarly light grey eyes regarded his wife with sardonic amusement.

'Most disturbing for you, my dear, but the invitation has already been accepted.'

'But, Matthew——'

'Must we argue?'

Clara Mendleson's stout body drooped. Her brown eyes had the expression of a wounded doe's. A touch of commonness—understandable since she had been Aldgate born and bred—did not detract from her popularity, although at times it enraged her husband.

In her early married life she had been happy with Matthew, but now they did no more than keep up appearances; and Clara had taken a strange, secret love of her own. Mendleson, knowing who the man was, took no apparent notice, content to play on his wife's nerves with covert innuendo.

He watched her sardonically as she turned from his over-luxurious study in their South Audley Street house.

'Clara, my dear, I hope I haven't interfered with any of your private arrangements?'

'No, no, of course not!'

She was panic-stricken as she hurried to her own room. But in five minutes she had taken a small white powder, in ten a hint of her earlier beauty returned and her eyes were shining.

Mendleson re-read Sharron's invitation.

'... to collect each piece under the same roof ... will be historic ...'

A quarter of a million pounds'-worth of jewels under one roof! The thought of realisable assets of such value had an unexpected effect on him. Forgotten were his dealings on the Stock Exchange, his company promotions, his involved financial commitments.

All the Kallinov collection would be at Beverley. Could he get them for himself?

11

'Oh, John will be there,' said Theo Crane lightly. 'I don't know about Lorna.'

His wife smiled. She was sitting at her dressing-table, brushing her long, lovely hair, and Crane stepped towards her. He was small, handsome, dark and quick-witted.

'We'll go, of course,' he said.

'We'd better, I suppose. As you put their antiquated ruin to rights we can hardly refuse to stay in it!'

'Quite a job that. I'm really proud of it. The strong-room was the most difficult. Sharron wouldn't have the jewels moved, and I was on edge until it was finished.'

It was two years since Crane, an architect who specialised in the reconstruction of old houses had 'modernised' *Beverley Towers*. His hobby was precious stones, and he owned the Rianti sapphires and the Kallinov rubies. It was his interest in jewels that had introduced him both to Sharron and to John Mannering.

Rene, married for ten years and in love with her husband, sometimes wondered whether she knew all that was in his mind.

'There's a note of acceptance from Fauntley this morning,' said Lord Sharron to his wife. 'Everything's turning out most satisfactorily. I've never wanted anything more in my life than to see that collection here!'

Lady Sharron's voice was sharp.

'I've no doubt at all that you'll try to buy the lot before you've finished.'

'Unfortunately that's out of the question,' said Sharron regretfully.

Tall, broad, inclined to put on flesh since his fiftieth birthday, Sharron lived for his hunting, his jewels and his position.

His wife was a magnificent-looking woman, tall, stately, deep-breasted, ruling the *Towers* with efficiency and arrogance. Of their two children, her favourite was their son; her daughter had roused her antagonism by getting engaged to a 'nobody', and Sharron was hardly aware that his own opposition to the match was inspired by his wife.

She had been worried by other things of late.

Though he had kept it from her, she knew that Sharron

had lost heavily on the stock markets, and was planning to start a new venture with Mendleson. She disliked Mendleson, but not strongly enough to offer opposition, if there was any chance of reviving the Sharron fortunes. Though faintly uneasy at their association, she knew that Sharron expected to create a big impression on the financier with the display of his own jewels.

They were, indeed, unique, even the hardened collectors being stirred at the sight of them arranged in the well-guarded library close to the strong-room. One might prefer diamonds to rubies, or emeralds to sapphires, but of their kind these gems were superb. The room seemed afire with the glory of the stones, and as John Mannering examined them—with Fay, Sharron's daughter—he was aware again of the temptation they presented.

He had suggested that it would be wise to have a special police guard, but Sharron had scoffed at the idea.

'I've two armed watchmen, and the strong-room is impregnable,' he said.

Mannering had seen the locks, the electrical control, and the alarm system, but knew that with the right tools not only he but any expert cracksman could get into the strong-room in an hour.

The *Towers* stood alone. Apart from cottages there was no house nearer than three miles. Three roads led from it, while in the grounds themselves, shrubs and copses afforded ample cover.

As the jewels were being taken back to the strong-room, Fay and her fiancé, a rather boyish and gloomy-looking man named Armstrong, slipped through a side-door into the garden.

It was cold. A bright half-moon showed up the white frost as it settled on meadows and hedgerows: the grass crunched sharply as Fay and Armstrong walked from the house.

Armstrong's head was bare. Fay, too, was hatless, the frost crisping the halo of her dark hair. Her face, small and piquant, looked worried.

'Bill, what's the matter?'

'Matter? Why, nothing.'

They walked without speaking past an ornamental lake,

13

now frozen over.

'Well, anyhow,' Armstrong said at last, 'if there is, it's nothing new. You know well enough that I'm nearly thirty, and no nearer to earning an income on which to marry you than I was two years ago. It's no use saying we can manage; you would never be happy on a pittance.'

'I can't *make* you get a licence, but one day perhaps you'll realise what a fool you are to waste precious years,' Fay said coolly.

Armstrong pushed his hand through his hair. With the collar of his coat turned up, his lean face with its high-bridged nose looked both handsome and obstinate.

'I suppose it's a form of snobbery,' Fay went on. 'If you would only realise how unimportant money is——'

'Unimportant? With a quarter of a million pounds'-worth of gems on display? On a tenth of that you and I could be far happier than any of the owners!'

'They're happy enough,' Fay said reasonably. 'Mendleson may live for money, but Crane is as much in love with Rene as I am with you, and Mannering——'

'That man! Why, he hasn't done a stroke of honest work in his life!' He looked away from her, and began to move towards the house. 'We'd better get back, you'll be frozen.'

Two men in the shrubbery crouched down, rubbing their numbed fingers, but forced to wait until the couple had returned to the house before they dared move.

Inside, Mannering was listening to Lord Fauntley.

'No, no, John!' Fauntley was saying testily. 'I can't agree. with you. Mongrel stones are interesting but not really valuable. The Glorias are exceptional because they were with the Kallinov collection. I won't have it said that a red diamond is worth three times a pure white.'

Fauntley raised himself on his toes to make the most of his stature. At sixty he had achieved an ambition: he was a Minister without Portfolio in the lately reshuffled cabinet. With it he had grown more self-important, more fussy, more self-opinionated; yet he remained at heart a friendly, likeable little man.

He would have continued the argument had not the first notes of Schubert's *Der Jangling und Der Tong* floated

14

softly through the long, high-ceilinged room.

At the end of it, Armstrong was the first to say good-night.

Mannering was about to follow suit when Sharron's son came in. Reggie Sharron was a tall, spindly youth who did not share his father's passion for precious stones, and had spent the weekend with friends.

Reggie lifted a casual hand in general greeting. Mannering chatted to him for a moment or two before going up to his room. The thought he took with him was that the Sharrons were anything but a united family.

He had no idea how long he slept.

It was still dark, and a light wind was blowing from an open veranda window when a sharp report disturbed him. It came again, a sharp clear sound, unmistakably that of a shot.

In a flash Mannering was out of bed, but before he had reached for his slippers, his door was flung open and Sharron appeared, a dressing-gown clutched unevenly, his eyes filled with alarm.

'Did you hear a shot?'

'I certainly did.'

'If anything's gone wrong I'll never forgive myself,' Sharron gasped.

Mannering turned abruptly towards the window. Pushing it wider open, he stepped on to a veranda. Against the grey, frost-covered ground he saw two men moving towards the drive.

CHAPTER TWO

ALARM

To Mannering's practised eye the wall on one side of the veranda offered a fairly good grip. Two feet to the right was a cement stone pillar, and this he gripped, letting himself swing from the veranda. For a moment he hung there, his whole weight on his arms as he felt with his feet for some slight support. Finding it, testing it, lost a precious minute and the sounds of the running men were almost out of ear-shot before he leapt the last four feet to the ground, and started off towards the drive.

Whether the shooting had been from Sharron's guards or from marauders, was anyone's guess.

Cries were coming from the house, and lights were springing up.

A little to his right, he saw a shadow moving in a shrubbery. He checked his pace, and made out the figure of a man moving through the maze of dwarf-trees.

The man was twenty yards or more ahead of him, and moving as fast as the shrubs would let him. Mannering followed warily, hoping that others from the house would catch up with him.

Suddenly, from his left, he heard the sound of a man's heavy breathing, then a breathless exclamation:

'Look out! There he is!'

There were obviously two men on his left, while the one he had been following was straight ahead. Mannering crouched low, knowing that the pair could see him clearly if he stood upright. Had the speaker referred to him or the man ahead?

'I can't see him.'

'He's foxing, damn him! Quiet!'

The whispers continued as Mannering moved cautiously forward, much hampered by the maze of shrubs. Without crashing through the bushes he could not be sure in which direction the path was leading him.

The frost was crunching beneath his feet, and he knew

that he could not prevent anyone near from hearing his approach.

Why didn't Sharron and the others come?

Suddenly the path ran into a clearing in the middle of the shrubbery. He could see a man, standing against the moon-lit sky, and recognised him as Erroll, Sharron's chief watchman. He saw the glint of a gun in the man's hand.

A second man seemed to appear from nowhere, behind Errol.

Obviously it was one of the two Mannering had over-heard, but his own sharp cry of warning was futile. A hand was raised, holding what looked like a truncheon, and it smashed down on the nape of Errol's neck. The watchman plunged forward, and the attacker dropped out of sight.

The voices were louder again.

'That's *that*, anyway.'

'Where's the other swine?'

'Never mind 'im—let's get a move on.'

At all costs Mannering wanted to stop the two raiders, and it seemed reasonable to assume that they would make for the drive.

He broke through the shrubbery as the two men appeared at the far end of it.

One was carrying a case, the other the weapon that had been used on Errol. They were running towards the drive gates, and they had one big advantage. Mannering was im-peded by a dressing-gown and slippers, while they were fully-dressed and well-shod.

The gates of the drive came in sight, and at the far side of the road beyond Mannering saw the sidelights of a car. There were fifty yards to go, and the couple had a twenty-five yards lead. The first man reached the car, wrenched open the door, and jumped in, pulling at the self-starter.

The second followed, flinging the case into the back. Mannering was now ten yards away, and his lungs felt like bursting. But if the escape was to be prevented it would have to be through him.

He jumped the last five yards, and as the car jolted for-ward, grabbed at the door handle. He could see neither of the men's faces, for they wore masks, but he caught the glitter of eyes as the window was opened, and the man next

17

to the driver lashed out with a length of solid rubber.

Excruciating pain shot along Mannering's forearm.

A clenched fist struck him in the chest and he was sent flying. Breathless and pain-racked, he fell to the gravel road. He did not see the rear light of the car disappearing, nor the four men who came rushing from the gates of the *Towers*.

Nor did he hear Sharron's high-pitched cry.

'Stop them—for God's sake, stop them—*they've got the jewels!*'

'What I can't understand,' said Mannering twenty minutes later, 'is why they came back.'

He was cushioned in an easy chair, pale-faced but not seriously hurt. Across his forearm was a weal already turning colour, but a strong whisky-and-soda had done much to restore him.

Servants had been set for Errol who, still unconscious, was lying on a couch near Mannering. Fay was sitting in an easy-chair, Rene perched on the arm. None of the other women had appeared, but Mendleson, Crane and the Sharrons were present, while Forbes hovered near the door. Neither Bill Armstrong nor Lord Fauntley had put in an appearance.

Mannering had been told what had delayed the party from the house.

Fay had raised the alarm, while her father had rushed to the strong-room. There was plenty of reason for Sharron to have lost his head: he had found the strong-room open, the Kallinovs and Alice's and Fay's personal jewellery missing.

Mannering's lips twisted wryly when he thought of the Glorias—of the *Baron* being robbed.

'We'd better get Errol round,' Sharron said heavily. 'He might know something.'

'Just what did you see, Mannering?' asked Mendleson. He seemed less disturbed by the robbery than anyone but Reggie Sharron, who appeared to judge it on its excitement value.

'Two men running hell-for-leather along the drive,' said Mannering. 'I went after them, but saw a third in the shrubbery. I thought it was one of the beggars, but it must have been Errol. That doesn't explain why the others came back. I wonder——'

'What?' asked Theo Crane quietly.

Mannering felt all their eyes on him.

'We-ell, the second time I saw them one of them had a case. The first time—I'm not sure. They might have planted the case in the shrubbery, and come back for it.'

'That still doesn't explain why they needed to put the case anywhere,' said Mendleson, kicking at the logs thrown hastily on to the dying fire. 'They must have had it to put the stuff in—so that suggests they carried the full case to the shrubbery, put it there, and returned to the house for some reason or other. Then you saw them, luckily, or we might have known nothing until morning.'

'Only the nearly-deaf could have slept through it,' Mannering said. 'Errol saw them first. You found his gun, didn't you, with two shots fired?'

Sharron had put Errol's colt ·45 on the mantelpiece.

'Of course.' Mendleson seemed confused.

'No bright deductive minds about here?' demanded Reggie.

'This isn't a thing to take lightly,' snapped his father. 'Have you sent for the police, Forbes?'

'Yes, sir.'

Two things were puzzling Mannering: the second watchman had not showed up, and Bill Armstrong had not joined the search party. Was either fact significant?

Mannering had seen with surprise that it was a little past two. He could not have been in bed much more than an hour before the shot had awakened him.

He was quick to see the implications behind that discovery even if the others failed. He knew that the three doors to the vault, and the safes, could not have been forced in less than an hour, which suggested that the work had been going on before he had retired, certainly before the whole household had been asleep.

The police would realise that, of course. It seemed to offer him a reasonable alibi, but not one which opponents of the Baron would consider sufficient.

He took a glass of water from Forbes, and held it close to Errol's mouth. The man stirred, and in five minutes he was

19

sitting up.

The full meaning of the situation did not at once strike him. When it did he tried to struggle to his feet.

'I—I *tried*, my lord! I——'

Mannering restrained him.

'We know you tried, Errol. What happened?'

It appeared he had been walking round the house—a regular hourly patrol—and had found the front door open. Then he had seen two men near the drive.

'I didn't see their faces,' he muttered. 'I went after them, fired at one, and I thought I was catching up when we reached the shrubs. I lost them there, and—and then something hit me. I think I wounded one man, me lord, but I don't remember anything after that.'

'Did either man have a case?' asked Mannering.

'I—I don't think so. I'm not sure.'

'What happened to Knowles?' asked Sharron sharply.

'Knowles?' asked Mendleson.

'The other watchman. He should be in the house. Forbes——' Sharron swung round. 'Have a search made of the house, quickly, but don't go near the strong-room. By the way, where's Fauntley? And'—he scowled suddenly— 'Armstrong? Did you call them, Fay?'

Fay stood up slowly, and every eye was turned towards her. Mannering felt the tension that had arisen.

'I didn't call Lord Fauntley,' she said clearly. 'I thought it best not to. I couldn't make Bill hear.'

Sharron stared, and then said heavily: '*Couldn't* you?'

The girl prepared to make a heated reply when Mannering broke in.

'I'm going to change, so I'll look in at his room. You and Mendleson are in better shape to assess the damage, Sharron. Theo, you'd better come and change, too.'

There was reason enough for them to get into warmer clothes, but as they went upstairs Mannering felt uneasy on Fay's account as well as his own. He hoped Armstrong had not been concerned in this, but he suspected that the others had jumped to conclusions, and that Fay was nervous.

If the clock was right, and his judgement on the quality of the strong-room accurate, somehow someone had helped from the inside: the theft could not have been done otherwise in the time. He felt his own sense of perception quickening in the urgent need of finding out the truth.

Before they had gone halfway up the stairs more evidence was forthcoming to suggest that the thieves had been working while the party had been in the music-room. Forbes, pallid and jittery, was coming from the kitchen quarters, and with him was an agitated and dishevelled man Mannering recognised as Knowles.

'What happened, Knowles?'

'I'm dreadfully sorry, sir. I—I—was going my rounds in the house when someone hit me over the head. Next thing I know, sir, I was tied hand and foot. Forbes just found me, sir. I—I must see his Lordship at once.'

Mannering glanced at Crane, who nodded, and they went back with the watchman. Sharron asked several sharp questions and dismissed the man in less than two minutes: then Mannering checked up on details.

Knowles had been attacked before midnight, which was all the proof of the time-factor that they needed. The use of the store-room seemed conclusive evidence that the attacker had known the house well.

'You get to bed, Knowles,' Mannering suggested. 'You'll be right as a trivet in the morning. Have some coffee sent up to my room, Forbes, will you?'

'At once, sir.'

Neither Mannering nor Crane spoke until they reached the landing at the top of the stairs. Looking down into the wide hall, with its marble statues and vast paintings, three centuries of the House of Sharron were revealed in a perspective that epitomised the stateliness of the *Towers* and the distinguished history of the family. As Crane spoke the soft echo of his words were lost in the high ceiling.

'Well, John, I wonder why Armstrong didn't wake up?'

Mannering shrugged.

'A heavy sleeper probably.'

'You don't seriously think so, do you?'

Mannering hesitated. They had reached Armstrong's door, but neither tapping or knocking brought any response.

Mannering tried the handle, and found that the door opened.

He saw at once that the bed had not been slept in, nor

21

was there any sign that Armstrong had undressed. Crane looked across at Mannering meaningly.

'It doesn't look too good for that young man, would you say?'

From the doorway Fay's voice cried out sharply:

'That's a beastly remark to make! Does he *have* to be the thief because he's missing?'

CHAPTER THREE

ENTER THE POLICE

Of the strength of the girl's love for Armstrong there was no room for doubt, and Mannering was prepared for an outburst of anger. But, strangely, none came. The architect hesitated, then stepped towards her.

'I'm sorry, Fay. I said the first thing that came into my head.'

'Yes, of course,' she said dully. 'The only difference between you and the others is that you said it, and they think it.'

Mannering sensed that she was afraid—and there was only one apparent reason for her fear. She, herself, was not sure that Armstrong was innocent.

'It's quite possible he heard something and went to investigate,' he said reassuringly. 'I doubt whether anyone is thinking he's involved.'

'Dad is, for one! The others—of course they are. They must do!' Her voice broke, there was a wealth of appeal in her wide grey eyes. 'He's not been to bed, his coat's missing, and—and he came up before anyone else.'

'Easy does it,' said the Baron, for he knew the girl was close to hysteria. 'This won't help Bill Armstrong. In point of fact——' He spoke more sharply, while Crane guided the girl to a chair. 'We've no justification for thinking anything,

22

and I was about to tell Theo he's talking out of the back of his neck. There was a car waiting at the end of the drive, and the thieves obviously used it. There isn't a tittle of evidence against Bill, any more than against Lord Fauntley. Why didn't you call him, by the way?'

' He had succeeded in steadying her.

'Well, he's too old to be out on a night like this, and I knew he'd dash off the moment he heard the jewels were gone.'

‗ She talked quickly and showed no inclination to go, while Mannering and Crane were shivering again, both anxious to get to their rooms and change. But neither of them had the heart to point that out to the girl.

· Mannering could not rid himself of an impression that she knew more about Armstrong's disappearance than she had admitted. He wished she would go, wished Crane would hurry to his own room. He wanted to think. How long would it be before the local police referred the robbery to Scotland Yard? What time would he have to prepare a 'defence' against the Yard's inevitable suspicion?

The ghost of the past was rising again, dangerous and insistent.

There was his own loss, too. The Glorias were well insured, but he valued them for their beauty, rather than for their worth.

At the back of his mind, also, was the thought of the scene which would come when Fauntley heard of the loss. The peer was jewel-proud to a point of mania. God, what a mess!

Someone tapped on the door.

Mannering looked up to see the small, grey, kindly figure of Lady Fauntley regarding him.

'I thought I heard—John what *is* the trouble? I've been lying awake for a long time trying to pluck up courage to come and see, but—my dear! You'll catch your death of cold and be in bed tomorrow with a temperature, you look frozen!' Her placid eyes regarded each one in turn, resting finally on Fay. 'Fay, do say something, what *has* happened?'

Mannering explained briefly.

'A robbery? Not all those lovely gems I hope—poor

23

Hugo will be so upset. John, I wish you and Mr. Crane would hurry along and change. Fay can tell me all about it.' She rested a hand on the girl's arm, while Mannering and Crane slipped out.

Mannering hurried to his room.

He bathed and dressed at high speed. There would be little opportunity of further sleep for some time.

His own problem now filled his mind.

Would there be talk of the Baron? It would be strange if he was not mentioned before the night was out. The fact that the Baron was reputed always to work alone would not prevent him being discussed; nor would it prevent the police considering him.

Damn the Baron!

Crane arrived as he finished, and they went downstairs together.

Sharron and Mendleson, neither of them changed, were the only two people in the lounge.

Sharron had aged in the past hour, every tinge of colour had gone from his face: but Mendleson looked his usual florid self, quite self-possessed and unflurried.

'If only I'd listened to you,' Sharron muttered again.

'Hang it, we're all insured,' Crane said.

'Insured!' Sharron shouted. 'They were the Kallinovs, no insurance could——' He steadied himself with an effort. 'Damn good of you to take it like this, but what will Fauntley say?' He hesitated, and his eyes hardened. 'Did you find Armstrong?'

Mannering shook his head.

'So it was he——'

'Now don't talk nonsense,' Mendleson said sharply.

He stopped, and all of them turned as the door was flung open, and Lord Fauntley appeared on the threshold. Nothing was left of the pompous, immaculate little man. He drew a deep breath as he stepped towards the men grouped about the fire. His voice was pitched high.

'Is—is it true, Sharron?'

'I'm afraid so,' said Sharron.

Fauntley flung his hands upwards.

'Gone! All gone! The Leopolds, the Dellings, the Kransits—gone!' He stood glaring, quivering with rage.

24

Mannering stepped to his side.

'You're not the only loser, Fauntley.'

Fauntley swung round, his face working.

'But you don't understand, those gems were priceless, the finest in my collection. I wouldn't lose them for a fortune! It's an outrage, where are the police, what are you doing about it? What—are—you—doing?'

Mendleson brought a tot of whisky. Fauntley drank it at a gulp, and some colour came to his cheeks.

'The police won't be long getting them back,' Mannering went on with seeming confidence. 'The Winchester men should be here at any moment.'

Hardly had he finished speaking when they heard the approach of a car. Mannering's heart thumped. The police. Would a Yard man be with them?

In less than a moment Forbes had opened the door to announce Chief Inspector Horroby of the Hampshire Constabulary. Mannering liked the look of his bright, direct blue eyes. Behind was an athletic-looking man of thirty or so, later introduced as Detective-Sergeant Glenn.

'Good evening, Horroby.' Sharron and the policeman were acquainted, obviously. 'Sorry to bring you out——'

'My job,' said Horroby briefly. 'Just what happened?'

He did not interrupt while Sharron gave a brief resumé of the night's activity, and his first request was to see Errol's gun. Using a handkerchief to prevent his own fingerprints being transmitted he opened it.

'Two bullets gone——'

'I've told you, Errol fired twice,' Sharron said, with a touch of irritation. 'Hadn't you better see the vault?'

'Yes, of course. I wonder if you gentlemen'—he looked at Fauntley, Mendleson and Crane in turn—'would mind writing a list of exactly what jewels you had in the safe, and a description of them? If you'll come with Lord Sharron and me, Mr. Mannering——'

Was there any ulterior motive in that request, wondered the Baron? There appeared no reason why he should go with the Inspector instead of one of the others. No sign of the alarm that shot through his mind showed on his face, and the trio left the room.

Horroby spoke before they reached the vault.

25

'I've heard something of you, Mr. Mannering. Inspector Bristow of the Yard is an old friend of mine.'

Bristow, one of the few men at the Yard who knew Mannering as the Baron, but could not prove it!

'We've met, of course,' Mannering was surprised that his voice was so steady, and angry with himself for being so full of nerves.

'Several times I gather,' continued Horroby. 'You gave him unofficial help, once or twice, didn't you? The Halliwell case last year, and that amazing Baron *alias* business——'

'Good lord!' exclaimed Sharron. 'I'd forgotten.'

His interruption gave Mannering time to assess the position. Bristow, then, had said nothing of Mannering being the Baron, and he felt more confident as they reached the strong-room.

The Inspector and Glenn examined the locks of the doors and safes carefully. Before they had finished, a second carload of police arrived. Flash-light photographs were taken, and fingerprint men set to work. There was a quiet, impressive efficiency about it all, particularly noticeable to Mannering.

Horroby frowned as he finished.

'If we three can have a chat without the others, I'd be glad, my lord.'

'Of course.' Sharron led the way to the small library where the display had been held a few hours before. Horroby looked gravely about him.

'As far as you've told me, my lord, the downstairs rooms were closed at half-past twelve. Is that right?'

'Yes. By then Forbes had shut the windows and retired.'

'And the first shot was heard at approximately one-thirty.' Horroby looked at Mannering as though seeing in him one more likely to understand what was coming than Sharron. 'I'm prepared to say, my lord, that the work on those doors was started about midnight. It was first-class Landon work, and would take an expert cracksman, with the proper tools for that type of lock, fully fifteen minutes each. No question of them being forced, of course, the marks of the tools are there.'

'But those locks should stand up to anything,' Sharron

26

protested.

Horroby grunted.

'Normally, yes. But whoever did this job knew the type of lock, and was able to get a skeleton key specially constructed to open them.'

'But, damn it, the makers——'

'You can't blame them,' interrupted Horroby. 'Every safe-making firm has to have these skeleton or master-keys. If you lost your keys, for instance, they would send a man with one of them, and he would get the doors open. Unfortunately, an expert safebreaker can examine a Landon lock—of this type—and get a special tool made as like a master-key as makes no difference. It means our men knew the type of lock, that's all.'

Sharron nodded, but did not immediately comprehend. Horroby glanced at Mannering, and then went on:

'Then the electrical control of the final door was cut—taking another fifteen minutes. After that, the three safes. Assuming there were two men, we can average the safes at ten minutes each, with the special tools mind you. That's an hour and a quarter's work, while the stuff had to be taken out and packed away. Altogether I would say that from the start of the burglary to the time Errol raised the alarm nearly two hours passed. It would be impossible for the work to have been done in much less time.'

Sharron was staring.

'But—good lord, that means it started before midnight, when we were all downstairs. It's impossible!'

Horroby shrugged, as if to say facts were facts.

'I'll have a locksmith's opinion in the morning, but I don't think there's much doubt. The very familiarity with the locks suggests someone who had an opportunity of examining them. Well now, I can't imagine a job of this size being done by local thieves, and it isn't wise to waste time. I'd like to call in Scotland Yard. The Chief Constable won't object, I'm sure, if you don't.'

Sharron still looked dazed.

'No, no, of course not. But you *can't* suggest there was help from someone inside the house!'

'But that is exactly what I am doing,' Horroby said grimly.

27

'Then—Armstrong——'

Horroby fastened on to the name, and Mannering held his peace, more concerned with that quick decision to consult the Yard. The shadows were closing in on him, and the devil of it was he could not prove that he had stayed in his room. It was useless for him to try to console himself with the fact that there had been plenty of witnesses to his chase after the thieves. Knowing the Baron, and bearing in mind the possibility that he had used accomplices, the police could say that his chase had been for effect.

And Sharron would be bound to disclose, sooner or later, that he had shown Mannering the whole system of the strong-room control.

Whether he liked it or not, he was at the heart of the inquiry, and would be among the Yard's first suspects. That problem would be solved if Armstrong's guilt was established, but he could not rid himself of a feeling that Armstrong's disappearance was due to a different cause.

Yet someone in the house had assisted in the robbery: Horroby had been quick to see that, and the Baron's knowledge of safe-breaking supported it. The special tools for the robbery had been essential, and from that someone the thieves had learned the essentials of the locks. Twenty-four hours would have been enough to get the keys made, a fact which meant each member of the house-party was a possibility.

If Armstrong was innocent, which one was it?

It was nearly half-past ten when Mannering left the breakfast room of the *Towers*.

He had managed to get five hours sleep before Chief Inspector Bristow of Scotland Yard arrived. The Inspector had acknowledged him politely—almost too politely—and asked for no interview.

Mannering had been on tenterhooks ever since.

The atmosphere at breakfast had been strained. The Mendlesons and the Cranes had been there, but the others had kept to their rooms—Reggie Sharron, it transpired, had a chill. Sharron himself had breakfasted early, with the two policemen.

Mannering went up to his room, expecting a call from

28

Bristow at any moment. Looking out of his window, he was confounding the robbery, trying to weigh up his own position——

Then he saw Fay.

She was walking away from the house, and he frowned as he snatched up a mackintosh and hurried towards the hall. Only Forbes was there, sorting the post, and he opened the door with a quiet good morning. Mannering nodded, and hurried out.

Fay was between the house and the shrubbery, walking towards a thick laurel hedge perhaps a hundred yards from the drive. Beyond the hedge, Mannering knew, was a sunken garden, a drop of fifty feet or more, approached by a steep path of crazy paving.

Mannering wondered whether he was jumping too freely to conclusions, but he could not rid himself of an idea that Fay might be meeting Armstrong. The thick hedge provided an excellent cover from the house and the drive, and his heart quickened at the thought that he might see the missing man.

She was walking along the narrow path at the top of the sunken garden which, shaded from the sun, was still white with frost. She turned, and saw Mannering.

Her start of surprise was genuine, and her cheeks flooded with colour as Mannering approached, without smiling.

'What—what are you doing here?'

'Following you,' said Mannering frankly.

'Why should you?'

'I wanted to find out whether you were meeting Armstrong.'

Her anger blazed.

'You too? I thought you were——'

'Well-disposed towards him? I am.' Mannering took out his cigarette case, and was glad when she accepted a cigarette. A match flared. 'Fay, it's no business of mine, but the police obviously suspect him.'

'The police aren't alone in that,' she retorted bitterly.

'No.' It was a damnable interview, but he sensed the girl's feelings. She was brittle and on edge, obviously fighting for fear that Armstrong was guilty. 'Fay, I lost heavily last night, but all the stones were insured and it isn't a loss to worry me much. I'm not after my pound of flesh.' He smiled, seeing the slight relaxation of her manner. 'You've some idea in your mind, and it's better shared.'

'I—I don't know what to say, to think!' She was very close to tears, and her voice was shaking. 'Bill was bitter about it all, that display last night made him mad, and I'm afraid he may have done some crazy thing.'

She broke off.

'I've been broke, Fay,' Mannering said. 'I know what it feels like.'

'*You?*' She looked startled. 'But that's absurd, he had only three hundred a year, nothing more. Father disapproved, made it clear that he thought Bill was after my money. I think sometimes he hated Father, would do anything to—to revenge himself.'

'Yes,' said Mannering. 'I know that feeling.'

She was beginning to believe him, although she could not read the thoughts in his mind, the memory of a day when a woman he had believed loved him had learned that he was comparatively poor, and the bitterness of her rejection had brought about the birth of the Baron.

'Bill was desperate! Last night he said he was going to get money, somehow. John——' She stepped towards him, her cold fingers trembled on his hand. 'I'm frightened! I feel like running away, so that the police can't make me talk, can't make me say anything that might hurt Bill.'

'It wouldn't help,' Mannering said quietly. 'Fay, if you're really stuck for someone to talk to, Lady Fauntley is the one.'

'But I hardly know her!'

'Try her,' Mannering urged. 'When the police have finished this morning, go to London with her. The party is breaking up, anyhow, and it'll be easily understood.'

She turned about quickly, to hide the tears in her eyes. Mannering stood silently, feeling desperately sorry for her.

He stopped thinking.

They were almost at the edge of the hollow, and he had glanced down, over the rymed, plant-covered rocks, and shrubs. At the bottom there was something else coated with white, and he recognised the huddled body of a man.

30

CHAPTER FOUR

FOUND

'Fay,' Mannering said quietly, 'what made you come here?'

She stopped crying: perhaps something in the tension of that question had made her respond at once.

'We—we often did. It's—secluded——' She had made a big effort, faced him, and saw his expression. 'John, what——'

He had been wondering whether to get her away on some pretext, but he decided that it would be wiser not to. From what he knew of her he believed she would take whatever was to come quietly, courageously.

'Someone's fallen over here,' he said quietly. 'I must go down and see who it is.'

She followed the direct of his gaze, her body rigid. She saw the fallen man, and gasped, but he knew he was right, for her voice had an altogether different tone.

'We'll both go down. There's a path, but it'll be slippery.'

She led the way to the edge of the hollow, where Mannering went in front of her. The path was dangerous, and they gripped shrubs and trees to help the descent. When they were at the bottom she hesitated, still staring at the cramped figure. She knew with Mannering that the chance of the man being alive was small. No one could have lived through the night lying there.

Mannering stepped forward. As he knelt down he saw the herringbone pattern of the light tweed coat, and knew that it was Armstrong's. One arm, bent in front of the face was stiff and difficult to move. He had it aside at last, and he saw two things at the same time.

It was Armstrong: and there was an ugly wound in the side of his head.

A bullet wound?

He was startled to find Fay standing immediately behind him when he turned, and there was no need for him to tell her. Her face had frozen into a mask of immobility. He put his arm round her in support and comfort.

'We'd better get help.'

Glancing up towards the top of the path he saw one of the plain-clothes police.

The man scrambled down to them.

'I've sent a man back to the house for help, sir. Is he dead?'

'I'm afraid so,' Mannering said. 'Can you manage? I'd like to get back.'

'If you'll just wait a minute, sir.' The man bent over Armstrong's body, and Fay turned away with a sharp intake of breath. An interval that seemed interminable passed before the man straightened up. 'I'm afraid you're right, we can't help him, sir. You'll be at the house?'

'Yes. Have you recognised him?'

'From the description given, sir, of the clothes, it seems like Mr. Armstrong.'

Mannering nodded, and turned away. He had to help Fay up the slope, and when they began the walk back to the *Towers* she went on blindly, sometimes stumbling, looking neither right nor left.

Although she had never allowed it to be known, several strange things had suggested to Lady Fauntley the possibility that Mannering was the Baron, and that Lorna knew it.

But she kept her thoughts to herself, and continued to look on Mannering as one of the family.

Her placid eyes held a hint of concern as Mannering spoke, and when he had finished she nodded quickly.

'Of course I'll look after her. I felt so sorry for her last night, so lonely I thought. What a pity her own mother—oh well, I shouldn't say things like it I suppose, and if she's disapproved of the engagement it' probably made things difficult, *such* a pity. And Sharon seems to be a little *unsound* over this business, John, don't you think? Where is she, dear?'

'In her room—I told her to expect you.'

Lady Fauntley's eyes sparkled.

'Isn't it strange how things happen when *you're* about, John? I remember three or four *remarkable* affairs,

32

although perhaps they happened first and you arrived after-wards,' She beamed. 'I'll go at once, and you might ring Portland Place and tell Parker we'll be back some time this evening. Hugo is still worrying about the jewels, and it would be an added annoyance to him not to have dinner ready.'

Mannering did as she had asked, tempted to ring Lorna also, but as he replaced the receiver and waited he saw that the drawer of the table on which the telephone was stand-ing was a little open.

Mannering stared at it, his lips pursed: he remembered very well, when he had last opened the drawer, closing it firmly.

He was frowning when he returned to the dressing-chest, and examined drawer after drawer.

For a long time he had been used to having his rooms searched, particularly at those times when the Baron had been busy, and the police had tried to find missing jewels at his flat. As he drew back from the chest, he knew that he had had visitors. A search had been conducted neatly yet hastily, and he needed no telling that Bristow had been at the bottom of it.

He could have found nothing, but it was confirmation of the way Bristow's mind was working, and as such made the need for finding the thieves more acute. Mannering poured himself a weak whisky-and-soda, and as he drank it slowly and thoughtfully there was a tap on his door. It opened before he could answer, and he was not surprised to see the neat figure of Chief Inspector Bristow.

Inches shorter than the Baron, who was six feet two, Bristow was something of a dandy. In his buttonhole was a pink carnation—Bristow without his flower was as un-thinkable as Clara Mendleson without her jewels. Frank grey eyes regarded Mannering watchfully.

Mannering steeled himself to show no concern.

'Hello, Bristow. Come in and close the door. The wind is positively whistling down the passages.'

He was watching the man lynx-eyed, but from Bristow's manner he judged that there was no immediate cause for worry, and his tension eased. Though Bristow had sworn to find evidence to convict the Baron, he would always fight fair. They possessed a mutual liking as strong as their mutual distrust.

'Can you spare me ten minutes, Mannering?'

'Of course. Sit down.'

Bristow accepted a cigarette and a drink. He had cause to be grateful to the Baron. Once he had saved his life; and twice he had enabled the police to make captures of considerable importance. If the Baron would only retire, for good, Bristow would be inclined to forget the past: but would the Baron ever really retire?

'Bill,' said Mannering, leaning an elbow on the mantelpiece and smiling, 'let us come into the open. Forget your assumption that I'm the Baron, and look on me as an ordinary citizen robbed of fifty thousand pounds'-worth of precious stones.'

Bristow stroked his moustache.

'I will say it doesn't *look* like a typical Baron job, Mr. Mannering.'

The Baron's tension eased.

'Nevertheless,' Bristow went on carefully. 'You were on the spot, and it's obvious Armstrong didn't do the whole job himself. For all I know you may have helped him.'

'I didn't. And why are you so sure that Armstrong was in it?'

Bristow shrugged.

'There isn't much doubt of that. He had a pocket-full of the smaller stuff—Lady Sharron's personal jewellery mostly—but I'm more concerned with the big stuff, and his accomplices. This was an expert job.'

Mannering said nothing. Through his own great relief came a picture of Fay's face as she had told that passionate story, and he knew how this discovery would affect her. On the face of it there was no doubt of Armstrong's complicity: the one thing the Baron had needed for his own freedom from suspicion seemed to have been presented to him, and yet——

Could Armstrong have known enough about the strong-room to have helped the thieves? It seemed unlikely. They *must* have had accurate information, and, more than probably, inside help. It was that fact, as clear to the police as to him, which explained his own anxiety.

34

'I'm hoping to prove,' Bristow said, 'that the bullets which hit Armstrong are those fired from Errol's automatic. They're the right calibre, and from the same gun. One lodged in his shoulder, and the other was found near where Errol first fired. It struck Armstrong's head first, I think. He went on to the hollow, getting away while you were preoccupied with Errol'—there was a hint of malice in Bristow's tone—'and the other two men.'

'Yes. But what made him fall, Bill? Or haven't you got that far?'

'I don't know. Miss Sharron tells me that he knew the garden well. Yet on a night when it was clear enough to read a newspaper he fell over the edge. Strange.'

'How badly would the wounds affect him?'

'The local surgeon says that neither would have rendered him unconscious. The fall doesn't fit in easily, Mannering. What did you know of him?'

'Practically nothing.'

'Everyone's the same!' Bristow said irritably. 'Here's a man engaged to the daughter of the house for two years, a familiar of several of the guests, and yet no one knows more than that he's an engineer in an obscure factory in London.'

'There's another puzzle,' Mannering said. 'We don't know why the two men visited the shrubbery twice.'

Bristow eyed him thoughtfully.

'We don't even know they did.'

Mannering forced his voice to keep steady.

'Meaning?'

'There isn't any need to beat about the bush,' said Bristow quietly. 'Your word isn't evidence I can rely on, Mr. Mannering. This is a queer affair: it doesn't look like the Baron, but that doesn't mean it wasn't you.'

'Can I never convince you that I'm not the Baron?'

Bristow lifted his hands impatiently.

'All right then, it doesn't mean it wasn't the Baron! The actual theft was thorough and typical of you—him. If it weren't for the fact that others saw the two men I'd doubt their existence. As it is I am doubting whether I've had a straight story from you.'

Mannering stood up.

35

'An appropriate moment for finishing the interview, I think.'

'No, it isn't,' snapped Bristow. 'I want to know what the girl told you.'

'You think my word's reliable there?'

'It can be corroborated,' said Bristow grimly.

Mannering hesitated, and then recounted his conversation with Fay. If Bristow had it from him, it might make it easier for the girl afterwards. But he was cursing the incvitability of police suspicion as he talked.

Bristow appeared to have forgotten their sharp exchange, and listened in silence, to say when Mannering finished:

'Yes. It gives a tenable theory, anyhow. He helped the thieves, took his share and started off alone. The kind of thing a young man with socialist tendencies might well do if he lost his head. But Errol shot him, and he knew he couldn't explain the wounds away, so he decided to end it.'

'Not a nice way of committing suicide,' said Mannering. 'There was the obvious risk of freezing to death.'

'Well, there's no other apparent explanation,' said Bristow abruptly, and Mannering knew that he was not satisfied. 'I can't understand why he didn't go off in the car with the others—that's the natural thing for him to have planned.'

'It's not, and you know it's not. The natural thing for him to have planned was to hide whatever jewels he had, and get back to the house. But if that *was* so, he couldn't return because Errol wounded him, and so the theory must be that he got to the Quarry and threw himself over.'

Bristow nodded without enthusiasm.

'Certainly he had the time, opportunity, motive; but dammit, you know how much stuff was taken. What I can't understand is why he was satisfied with trinkets. It's reasonable proof that he helped the thieves, But it wasn't much pay.'

Mannering shared Bristow's doubts. Would a man in Armstrong's position endanger everything he possessed and loved for such a small reward? He said thoughtfully: 'If we assume that he had more when he left the house, we're also saying it's possible that he was pushed over.'

36

Bristow changed the subject, too abruptly to be convincing.

'Well, what are you going to do about your supposed loss?' he asked.

'How childish you are, Bill. Naturally I'm going to wait for the police to get it back for me.'

Bristow said sourly: 'Well, if you're *not* in this thing, don't start working on your own. If you do, we'll get you before you've properly started.'

'Think so? After all, every man has a right to look for his own property, and I was fond of the Glorias. I bought them from Galinet of Paris; if you'd care to see the receipt call at Brook Street any time. However, I'll probably be too busy.'

'You'd better be,' said Bristow grimly.

He left Mannering soon afterwards, and the Baron sat back in an easy-chair to take stock of the situation. The evidence pointed strongly to Armstrong's complicity: he did not know enough of the young man to believe one thing or the other about him, but it was significant that Fay should not put the theft past him.

Yet was it likely he would have taken such a risk for five or six thousand pounds'-worth of jewels with a 'stolen goods' value of less than half that sum? No wonder Bristow was uneasy!

There was another point. Bristow might doubt his story, but the two men *had* turned back. Supposing the whole robbery had been finished before Errol saw the thieves? Supposing the two men he had nearly stopped had put the bulk of the haul in the case, left it in the shrubbery and gone back to see Armstrong? Supposing Armstrong had had other jewels but been robbed of them in turn?

Was it not possible that they had been with him when he had been shot? They could have pushed him over the edge, knowing he had stuff enough to incriminate him. The plentiful trees and shrubs would have hidden them from Errol, who admitted he had lost them—as Mannering had done later.

Had there been time for that, between the shooting and the moment he had looked out of the window?

Three minutes would have been ample—and Sharron had delayed him that long, if not more. It seemed likely to be generally assumed that Armstrong had committed suicide; would the police rest on that assumption?

Could *he* find the truth, and at the same time the Glorias?

He stood up, trying to force the thought away from him. Bristow was right, he would be a fool to meddle with the business. He might try to trace the stuff, through fences known to the Baron, but that must be the limit of his activities. The Baron was dead, and had to stay dead.

He felt the old, familiar pull towards the Baron, the call for action. There was the thrill of a chase, too, and something of the fire that had started the Baron on his brief, exhilarating career came back: if he acted on impulse he would be in the middle of the affair before he knew what had happened, despite Bristow's warning.

'Keep right out of it,' Mannering said virtuously. 'Yes? Come in.'

Forbes entered his room with letters in his hand.

'I thought you would like your post, sir.'

'Oh yes, thanks.'

Mannering glanced at them. One was from Lorna. He read it first, and stood musing for a few minutes afterwards, with the letter in his hand.

The second was from *Kingleys* of Hatton Garden. The Wellborough emeralds were on the market, and Mr. Mannering had expressed his interest in them some while before. Was he still interested? Mannering made a mental note to call on *Kingleys*; and opened the third letter, also typewritten.

And then he stared down, narrow-eyed, at the last thing he had expected—a challenge and a threat to the Baron, startling in their abruptness.

'What's it feel like, Baron? And won't Bristow be glad when he finds you've got the Kransit diamonds?'

CHAPTER FIVE

CHALLENGE?

'And won't Bristow be glad when he finds you've got the Kransit diamonds?'

The first sentence was unimportant, everything else which had happened faded into insignificance when compared with those thirteen words. Even the fact that someone who had been a party to the burglary knew him as the Baron seemed not to matter.

The first moment of realisation brought him almost to a pitch of panic, and the colour drained away from his cheeks. He felt his fingers trembling, saw the letter shaking. His earlier fears had not been groundless, then. He was in acute danger.

He had no idea where Fauntley's Kransits were, but the letter implied that they were likely to be found somewhere likely to incriminate him.

The first possibility was that they had been hidden somewhere in his room, but he pushed it aside quickly. They were not at the *Towers*, for the police had already made a search of his room, and Bristow would have acted by now if he had found them. The only other likely place was his Brook Street flat.

The thieves could have put them there quite easily—but why had they warned him? Why had they not let Bristow search the flat, make the discovery, and pounce on the Baron? A word to the police would have ensured an immediate search at Brook Street.

One idea occurred to him. In all probability they would prefer to keep away from the police, even from telephone contact. But they might intend to lure him from the *Towers*, tempt him to make a fast run to London, knowing that he would be watched, and in all likelihood followed. It seemed almost too ingenious, but it was a tenable theory.

The possibility made him sweat.

If the Kransits were at the flat and he moved from the

Towers with any apparent haste, it would be an open invitation to Bristow to telephone Scotland Yard. The resultant police visit to the flat would be over before he was halfway to London.

'It's clever,' he muttered, 'it's a damned sight too clever. And it's an even bet that Bristow is having these telephones tapped.'

There were four exchange lines from the *Towers*, and three of them had extensions, but if the police were listening-in it would be done from outside, so that no one at the *Towers* would have reason to suspect it. He had to get to a telephone free from all risk of police surveillance, and he hurried out.

No one was in the passage, but Crane was alone in his room, looking through a magazine.

'Hello, John, in a hurry?'

God, thought Mannering, I'm showing it as clearly as that! Aloud he laughed.

'Yes and no, Theo! I'm fed right up with staying in. What about a brisk walk?'

Crane was ready, and five minutes later they were heading for Beverley. So was a plain-clothes man, as Crane remarked with a grimace.

'To be suspect is an experience anyhow. That man Bristow obviously thinks that there's an accomplice in or near the *Towers*. I saw him go into your room, by the way, what did he have to talk about?'

'You're right about his views on an accomplice, but apparently Bristow had decided that he—if it is a he—is no longer at the *Towers*. These flatfoots are behind us merely as a matter of form.'

'A consolation,' said Crane. 'To lose the Riantis and the Kallinov rubies one night, and be in jail for stealing them the next, isn't my idea of a joke!'

Half an hour's brisk walking had brought them to the outskirts of Beverley. They had passed a telephone by twenty yards when Mannering turned sharply on his heel.

'Damnation! That reminds me—Lorna was thinking of coming down this afternoon, and she won't want to land in this mess, I should have phoned her before. How are you for change?'

Crane found some sixpences and coppers, and watched Mannering curiously as he turned to the kiosk.

In three minutes Mannering heard Lorna's deep voice at the other end of the wire.

'Hallo?'

'Lorna, darling,' said Mannering quickly, 'this is going to be serious. Can you go out at once?'

He heard the quick intake of her breath.

'Yes—I will do. What's happened?'

'A burglary here, and some stuff planted at Brook Street, I suspect. Will you get there, look round thoroughly, and if you find the stuff telephone Leverson to send a man for it?'

'Yes,' said Lorna.

'Bless you! I—on second thoughts, phone Leverson from the studio and ask him to send a man to Brook Street at once, the said man to call every quarter of an hour; that will make sure he's at hand if you want him. I'll get up as quickly as I can.'

'Is it dangerous?' Lorna wanted to know.

'I wish I knew,' said Mannering with feeling.

He sensed Lorna's anxiety, but there was little he could do to reassure her: he hated the fact that he had to incur the risk of her being involved, but a search at the flat without loss of time was essential. He left the kiosk, smiling cheerfully and apologetically at Crane.

Crane claimed that he was feeling hungry.

They made their way back to the *Towers*, and as they neared the drive they saw Bristow's Morris 12 turning from the gates. Bristow raised a hand in salute, and drove past. Mannering, his nerves on edge, saw danger in the Yard Man's early departure, but forced himself to act as though there was nothing on his mind.

At the *Towers* he was in a quandary.

Bristow had left for London, and Horroby had returned to Winchester, leaving Glenn in charge. The guests were free to leave when they liked, and most of them were going immediately after luncheon.

On the surface it was satisfactory enough, but had Bristow sent a message for his, Mannering's, flat to be searched? Did he know anything about the suggestion that

41

the Baron had the Kransits?

It was an unbearable hour, and Manner was sweating when at last he tok leave of the others and, driving alone in his Lagonda, left for London. He drove fast, the fear of impending disaster at his heels, and after averting a collision by a hair's-breadth, he muttered aloud:

'This won't do, damn you! Get a hold of yourself.'

He forced himself to consider the possibility of Armstrong's accomplice—assuming Armstrong was guilty in part, which seemed established—being one of the guests, or even one of the Sharron family. The same unknown knew him for the Baron, and that narrowed the issue.

Fauntley? Most unlikely. That narrowed it down to Sharron, Mendleson and Crane.

He remembered that Mendleson had been less perturbed than any of the victims. But Mendleson, reputed to be one of the ten richest men in England? No, it was absurd!

Crane and Sharron seemed equally unlikely.

He frowned, for he had forgotten young Reggie. He knew him well enough: once or twice when the Baron had been busy he had cursed Reggie Sharron for calling at his flat. He recalled that Reggie was frequently in need of money, and when borrowing complained that his father was tight-fisted. Reggie was twenty-seven, old enough to have a reasonable allowance, but he did not get it. Nor was Sharron anxious for his son to do anything but assist in the management of the Beverley estate.

Taking the facts as they appeared on the surface, Reggie was the most promising suspect. A hard-up, rather stubborn and self-willed youngster with a grievance.

Yet it was Mendleson's face which kept appearing in front of Mannering's mind's eye. Awareness of the financier's peculiar reputation in the City would not fade. Mendleson was reputed always to get what he wanted.

Had he wanted the Kallinovs?

It was not a question of finding the actual thief among the house party, but simply a matter of finding whether the thieves had been inspired by one or the other of the five men. Mannering was compelled to admit that himself apart he could not be positive that any one of them was clear.

He reached the Great West Road, and thereafter the

traffic kept him too busy to puzzle the situation out. As he neared the West End something of the earlier panic returned: it grew into an obsession, and when he swung into Brook Street he scanned each side of the road for plain-clothes men.

He saw one, and he jammed on the brakes so hard that the Lagonda jolted him forward against the windscreen.

There was no mistaking the gangling, melancholy Sergeant Tring. Tring was so obviously a policeman that his calling could be recognised in an instant. His speciality was fingerprints and searching, and he was Bristow's regular *aide*.

Tring ambled towards the car, and Mannering steeled himself to talk lightly.

'Hallo, Tanker, after some more bad men?'

'Always plenty of *them* about, Mr. Mannering. Been away?'

'Of course you can't guess where I've been,' retorted Mannering.

'Come to think, I do remember something about being at Beverley,' said Tring with a near approach to a smile. 'What a do! Matter o' fact, Mr. Mannering, there's a suspicious character been calling at your flat on and off today.'

Tring jerked his head, and Mannering glanced along the pavement to see a short, thin man looking at the numbers of the houses as though in search of a port of call. Mannering did not recognise him, but he guessed that he was Flick Leverson's man. Leverson, a fence extraordinary, was a good friend of the Baron's.

But Leverson had failed him by sending a man Tring recognised.

'Called three times,' said Tring confidentially. 'I thought you ought to know.'

Mannering turned towards the house, and his first-floor flat. Tring walked by his side.

'I'd better make sure everything's all right, sir, we don't want to you to lose any *more* stuff, do we?'

Sarcasm from Tring was so rare that Mannering knew there was something behind it. Did Tring *know* why the other man had come, and who he was from? Had the flat already been searched, and was there a trap waiting for him

43

when he reached it?

The temptation to turn tail and fly assailed him, but he showed nothing of it as he inserted the key in the lock, Tring at his shoulder.

The flat seemed in perfect order, and there was no sign of Lorna. Mannering closed the door, and stepped through to his bedroom.

Tring looked in the doorway.

'Everything O.K. here, Mr. Mannering?'

'You might look under the bed for me, Tanker,' murmured the Baron.

Tanker Tring, least imaginative of men, went down on his knees and lifted the coverlet of the bed. It would have been amusing but for the fact that Mannering was aware of a faint, lingering perfume, immediately recognisable as Lorna's.

So she had been here.

And Leverson's man was still outside, which suggested she had found nothing.

He saw her suddenly.

She was pressing close against the wall, on the far side of the wardrobe, tall, dark, dressed with simple perfection, her flawless skin given greater emphasis by her luxuriant dark hair. Some said that her expression was too close to sullenness for her to be called beautiful, but Mannering would have none of it; pretty she was not, but beautiful she certainly was.

And now there was an expression of urgency, of alarm, on her face.

Mannering was on tenterhooks, afraid that Tring would go further into the room: if he saw Lorna he would know there was something wrong.

'I suppose everything *is* O.K.,' said Tring. 'I——'

Mannering went rigid, staring into the living-room. Tring followed his gaze, and Mannering's voice was no more than a whisper.

'Did that handle turn?'

Tring stepped towards the door, and Mannering followed him. Cautiously they crept through, towards an imaginary intruder.

Mannering's heart turned over.

44

For someone was there, opening the outside door of the flat, and as they approached he saw Bristow. Bristow ·and Tring together could mean only one thing.

He looked steadily towards the Inspector, who nodded curtly. Out of the corner of his eye Mannering saw Tring shake his head, very slightly.

Bristow's voice was sharp, abrupt.

'Mr. Mannering, I've information that you have some of the Kallinov jewels in your possession.'

Mannering stared.

'You've *what*?'

'Don't hedge,' snapped Bristow. 'I want to see what's in your pockets.'

The Baron returned Bristow's frosty gaze with one equally cold.

'Bristow, this is going too far. I haven't been here five minutes, and I've had the escort of your little man all the time——'

'I know all about that. They weren't in your room at the *Towers*, but you were followed from there, and you were also seen telephoning from a kiosk. The inference is that you have the stones with you—and another inference,' Bristow added grimly, 'is that you were going to hand them to Leverson's man, outside. Well, you won't—he's being watched.'

Mannering was wondering how much of this Lorna was hearing, praying that she would get out by way of the fire-escape. But there was the possibility that the police were watching the back as well as the front of the house; if she did get away she might be detained: which would mean disaster, for by her expression he guessed that she had found the Kransits.

Had the police been watching when she had arrived?

He spoke in a deceptively mild voice.

'The little matter of a search warrant, Bristow.'

'Why waste the time? You know I can get one for the asking.'

Mannering shrugged, as though he had decided that capitulation was the wisest course. He saw Bristow's eyes, hitherto hard and wary, show surprise, and he knew he had been expecting stronger opposition. Yet by letting them look through his pockets he would be giving Lorna time to get away.

Mannering was satisfied that the conclusion he had drawn from the anonymous letter was not far out: Bristow had been given the information about the Kransits in time to watch him at the flat, but not before. He could not hope to learn where the information had come from then.

Tring did a thorough job.

The jumble of oddments from Mannering's pockets grew, proportionately with the length of Tring's face. Despite the fact that within two minutes he must have been sure that the diamonds were not on the Baron, he spent fifteen minutes turning out every pocket, examining every lining. Not until then did he give up, while Mannering eyed Bristow with veiled mockery.

'Apologies are due, I think.'

'You had the jewels——'

'Don't be a damned fool,' snapped the Baron. 'You told me that I'd been under observation from the moment I left the *Towers*, you know I've had no opportunity of getting rid of anything. I didn't touch the Kransits, Bristow. Next time I shouldn't put so much trust in a squealer.'

He was feeling relieved up to a point, but the danger to Lorna still seemed acute, and until he knew what had happened to the Kransits there would be no peace. There was some satisfaction in finding Bristow at a loss for words, and even stumbling into an apology. But when the ring came at the front door bell he was tense again ready for any revelation as Tring opened the door.

Lorna came in!

She was smiling, and there was an assurance in her manner that sent relief sheering through the Baron. She was almost coquettish with Bristow, and when the door finally closed behind the policeman Mannering gripped her arms tightly.

Eyes and lips smiled close to his.

'No trouble,' she said, 'but when Tring came in I nearly collapsed! I'd found them underneath the wardrobe, a minute before you arrived. I'd seen Tring outside, so I didn't call for Leverson's man. Thank God the fire-escape wasn't watched!'

46

'Where are they now?'

'I gave them to a cabby to take to Leverson's flat, and phoned him to expect them.'

The Baron began to laugh.

Lorna joined in, but they sobered to the realisation that danger still existed. Bristow was not likely to be fully satisfied until the mystery of the *Towers* robbery was solved.

The question was—would it be solved? And would the thieves make further efforts to incriminate the Baron?

That question, with the other problems, left him no chance but to start the chase independent of the police.

CHAPTER SIX

FLICK LEVERSON

In a house in Wine Street, Aldgate, lived that doyen of fences, Flick Leverson. Leverson had bought and sold stolen jewels for forty years, and in the 'trade' was of unblemished reputation. He was past sixty, and already conservative about his clients. One of the few for whom he continued to work was John Mannering.

In the past Leverson had helped the Baron out of many a tight corner, and thus their friendship had been forged. A tall man, with his left sleeve hanging empty from a war-wound, grey-haired, cultured, mellow, he would have been at home in any exclusive London club. His steady, occasionally twinkling grey eyes, his deep, pleasing voice, were those of gentleman born. On either side of him at Aldgate lived general practitioners, who had not the faintest idea of their affable neighbour's true calling, thinking him only a collector of priceless antiques.

All of this Bristow, who had arrested Leverson on the occasion of his only trial and prison sentence, knew well, knowing also that Leverson was as difficult a man to catch

47

as the Baron.

On an evening two days after the robbery at the *Towers*, Leverson sat in a comfortable chair, a brandy glass in his hand. Opposite him was Mannering, equally at ease.

'And so,' Mannering said, 'I can't keep out of it, Flick. I want the Glorias back, I want to find how far Armstrong was involved, and I want most of all to find who tried to put me away.'

Leverson spoke reluctantly.

'It might prove nasty, John. Bristow won't let up now he thinks you have fooled him. I'm devilish sorry about sending a man Tring recognised; I thought he was safe.'

'The Yard must be getting more proficient,' Mannering said sardonically.

'I needn't warn you not to under-rate them,' returned Leverson. 'They were here within an hour of the Kransits arriving, but I had the gems safely away, of course. Do you want them now?'

'There's plenty of time.'

'And that settles that,' said Leverson with a shrug. 'Well, now, you say the letter was typed at the *Towers*?'

Mannering lit a cigarette, and eyed Leverson thoughtfully.

'More, Flick. It was typed on a machine in Sharron's small library, accessible to anyone, family, servant or guest. It was posted *before* the robbery, which means whoever sent it was confident of success. And although I can just believe Armstrong would help in the robbery, I don't believe him capable of trying to plant the jewels on me, nor arranging for it to be done. There's a vindictive man behind this, and a clever one, and he isn't going to be pleased that I escaped trouble. Worse, he knows I'm the Baron, and I can't be sure what he'll try next. However,' added Mannering grimly, 'he is not likely to rejoice in his efforts for long, if I have any say in the matter. Well, will you keep your eyes and ears open for the rest of the Kallinovs?'

'Yes.' Leverson frowned. 'I don't know whether they'll cut up a collection like that, though, they might have a buyer for the lot. I'll watch, anyhow. Is that all you want?'

'Yes and no,' said Mannering. 'Rightly or wrongly, I've narrowed the suspects down to Mendleson, Crane, Fauntley and young Sharron. I'm sticking to men. Fauntley and Crane seem impossible, but—well, have you heard anything of Mendleson and Reggie Sharron?'

Leverson frowned.

'I can't say I have, John. Mendleson's a local product, you know, he was born in Whitechapel High Street. He's not a man I like.'

'Do you know him?'

'Quite well. He has one of the finest collection of seventeenth-century French cabinet work in the world. I've been to his place several times, and he's been here.' Leverson nodded towards a superbly carved silver table. 'He's after that, of course, with a no-limit cheque if I would sell. He has a queer reputation I'll grant you, and is the stop-at-nothing type. I'll make what inquiries I can, and ring you. But for God's sake, be careful!'

Mannering laughed, finished his brandy, and departed.

The brandy had warmed him, but the night was bitterly cold—the fourth day of that cold spell which had ended in disaster for Armstrong. The youngster had fallen—or been pushed—and lost consciousness: probably he had not felt the coming of death, from exposure, and contributed to by loss of blood. The inquest had been adjourned after the briefest of hearings. Mannering could not keep his mind off the affair, off its various ramifications. He turned to the right, and as he did so he caught a glimpse of a man standing, cold, miserable and familiar, outside Aldgate Station. He made a bee-line for him.

'Hallo, Tanker, still at work?'

'Indeed, yes, sir. I forget what an armchair feels like. On a night like this, too, enough to freeze you stiff.'

'A drink seems indicated,' said Mannering cheerfully. ·

'Not me, sir. Duty's duty.' Detective Sergeant Tring sniffed.

'Incorruptible member of an incorruptible police force,' said Mannering. 'You might tell Bristow I've just been on a social call, and I'm going straight to my flat.'

He nodded, smiled, and as a taxi came near, lifted a hand. Before Tring had a chance of getting a second one, Mannering was inside. By the time the disgruntled Inspector had found a taxi, Mannering's was out of sight. Tring

49

gave orders to be driven to 88g, Brook Street. If Mannering *was* going straight home there was no damage done.

Mannering did, in fact, go directly to his flat. The fact that Tring had been on his trail meant that Bristow was taking no chances. It was not going to be easy to play a lone hand.

The brightest spot, so far, was that Fay Sharron had found friends in Lorna and Lady Fauntley.

After the guests had left the *Towers* there had been a family quarrel, unnecessarily bitter on her parents' side. Fay had left at once, and gone to the Fauntleys' Portland Place house. Whether it would mean a breach between the Fauntleys and the Sharrons was not of particular importance. The importance lay in Sharron's outspoken condemnation of Armstrong.

Was Sharron *glad* to find a scapegoat?

A second result of the burglary had been the dismissal of Errol and Knowles, the watchmen. They had done, apparently, everything that could be reasonably expected of them; nevertheless, they had been dismissed as soon as the police had given permission. It would go hard with them to find other work, although both were pensioned C.I.D. officers, likely to suffer no acute hardship.

A man who usually took the bad with the good, and who was not easily angered, should not have lost his head as Sharron had done. His own culpability—or what he called his own—might have explained it in some measure of course, but was it a sufficient explanation?

Mendleson—the Sharrons—Crane.

All with equal opportunities.

No, that wasn't true. The Sharrons had the best opportunities, knowing exactly what type of locks were used. But the whole affair was such a maze of complications and contradictions that only the anonymous letter could be called reliable evidence.

Now that Leverson was on the watch, however, word might come through.

As he opened the door Mannering heard the *brrr-brrr* of the telephone, and stepped towards it. Lifting the receiver he heard the voice of Reggie Sharron, still thick and hoarse.

'Hallo-oo! Is that you, Mannering? ... I've been trying

50

to get you all the evening. I've got to see Fay, and she won't
have anything to do with me. I've got to see her——'

'Why?' asked Mannering, sharply.

'Better not babble over the telephone.'

'Can you come round here?'

'Not a hope. This stinking cold. I'm told I ought to be in
bed. Can you come here? I'm at the Junior Reserve.'

'I'll be over in twenty minutes,' promised Mannering.

When he reached the street he saw that his own cab had
gone, and that Tanker Tring was paying off another. The
Baron's eyes gleamed as he stepped to the kerb.

'Hallo, Tanker, clues lead you this way? You've
brought just what I wanted. The Junior Reserve, cabby,
please.'

Tring, muttering highly-coloured imprecations, espied
another taxi a hundred yards away, and lumbered towards
it.

Mannering reached the Junior Reserve Club ten minutes
after receiving Reggie's call. A page-boy took him to the
fourth floor, which was also the cheapest, further evidence
that the peer kept his son on short commons.

A thick voice called, 'Come in.'

Sharron started to struggle to his feet, as a cough shook
his whole body. Mannering was alarmed by his feverish
flush.

'Don't get up, you idiot, and why the blazes aren't you in
bed?' Mannering demanded. 'What the devil brought you
from Beverley like this?'

Reggie attempted a smile.

'Oh well, brotherly love and all that kind of thing. Sorry
about this sniffing. I—at-choo!' He sneezed four times, and
was gasping for breath when he finished.

'I'll give you a hand to get in bed,' Mannering said.
'Have you a regular doctor in town?'

'Oh, all right, old Gregory of Queen Anne Street—you
know him.'

In ten minutes Sharron was in bed, packed with hot-
water bottles, and the doctor, Mannering hoped, on his
way.

'S-sorry to be such a p-pest,' gasped Reggie as he settled
down. 'My head's going like a trip-hammer! I—Lord, I

51

forgot. Look here, Mannering, I really ought to see Fay, she—well, I mean she ought to know.'

Something of Mannering's earlier tension returned, but he spoke casually enough.

'Ought to know what?'

'Well, about Bill, y'know. I——' Another interval for sneezing, and then Sharron gasped his story out. 'One of the maids did the room next to Bill's late that night. It had got missed or something, oh yes, a hot-water bottle leaked, and they couldn't let Mrs. Crane sleep in wet sheets.' He forced a ghost of a grin. 'She says she saw Bill go into his room at a quarter-past twelve, and heard him walking about for ten minutes. And when she was there ten minutes later, just before the Cranes went into the room, he was still there— he poked his head out and asked if she'd seen Fay. What I mean, Mannering, is that he couldn't have been fooling— ooh, my head!—about with the safes *and* in his room, could he now?'

Mannering looked at him narrowly. If Armstrong had not been helping the thieves, how had he been shot?

A possibility flashed through his mind, one that seemed to explain many things. Supposing Armstrong had gone out, seen the thieves and been mistaken for one? Supposing they had doubled back, dodged Errol and planted the jewels before pushing him into the sunken garden?

It was a fresh angle altogether, opening out the possibility that Armstrong was not concerned at all, and it sharpened Mannering's appetite for the chase.

Mr. Cornelius Gillison, of Barnes, glared at the scared face of a man in front of him.

'You damned fool! You put that stuff in Armstrong's pocket, when I told you to get it and come here straight away. Everything was fixed, and you——'

'We—we 'ad to finish him! Before 'e was shot 'e'd seen——'

'Never mind who he saw! Listen, Smith, get rid of that stuff, or some of it. D'you hear? If you don't you're through. And next time I send you out on a job, follow instructions or I'll break your blasted neck!'

52

And while Smith sidled away, Gillison flung himself in a chair and tried to solve the problem that the incrimination of Armstrong had created. Presenting the police with one suspect had its dangers; putting up two was madness.

CHAPTER SEVEN

COMPLICATIONS

The doctor looked sternly up at Mannering outside Reggie Sharron's door.

'We mustn't move him. I'll arrange for a day and night nurse. Pleurisy, without doubt, and he had a nasty spell of it last year, we don't want a pneumonia case if we can help it. I'll get in touch with his father.'

Mannering spent five minutes with the secretary of the Junior Reserve and felt sure that there would be no lack of attention for Reggie. Outside, standing between two street lamps brilliant in the frost was Tring. Mannering had long passed the stage when Tring was a joke. He said sharply:

'Ask Mr. Bristow if he can be at my flat in half an hour, Sergeant, and tell him it's in connection with the Sharron burglary.'

Tring wavered uncertainly. He knew how deeply Bristow felt about the burglary in Hampshire, and was torn by the responsibility of deciding whether to follow Mannering or whether to lose time by telephoning Bristow's Chelsea house.

Mannering's uncompromising back, and his clear voice instructing a cabby to go to Portland Place, decided him. Tring went to the nearest call-box, and Mannering saw him pulling the door open as he went by in the cab.

Parker, Fauntley's butler, opened the door at Portland Place.

' 'Evening, Parker. Is Miss Lorna in?'

'Yes, sir, in her lounge with Miss Sharron.'

Standing with her back to a blazing log fire, her cheeks flushed with the heat of the room, Lorna looked her best. It was always difficult for Mannering to believe that this tall, lovely, sometimes passionate creature was the child of Hugo and Lucy Fauntley.

'You needn't worry on that score, Fay,' she was saying. 'If you're right, and Bill Armstrong was victimised by someone else, John will find out.'

She broke off as Mannering entered the room.

He greeted them with a smile, adding: 'I haven't many minutes, I'm afraid, but I thought Fay ought to know that Reggie's at the Club, running a spot of temperature. Dr. Gregory says there's no need to worry.'

It was hard to understand the expression in Fay's eyes.

'What made him come to town?'

'He told me he wanted to see you.'

'Yes,' she flashed, 'with a message from home I expect. "Come back, all is forgiven, the villain is dead!" I won't go back. They've been beasts, all of them, and I'm staying here!'

'That's the spirit,' Mannering said easily, and he decided on the instant to say nothing of Reggie's story; she was in no mood to be encouraged by what might prove to be a false hope. He told her he had opened several lines of inquiry, and left it at that.

He went off thoughtfully, to find Bristow waiting outside his flat. He shook hands affably enough, as he said:

'I hope this means you're working with me, Mannering.'

'As far as I can,' said Mannering, 'but Tring's had an unhappy evening, I'm afraid. Well now, Bill'—they were settled in front of the electric fire—'you questioned the maids at the *Towers*, of course?'

'Yes.'

'Any story that was interesting?'

'They were a dull lot,' admitted Bristow, who had no objection to giving Mannering general information. 'Why?'

'Reggie Sharron's in London, down with pleurisy, and he won't be able to talk sense, I fancy, for some days. But he gave me a garbled story of a maid who says she was in the room next to Armstrong's, and saw him there at the time the

54

robbery must have been under way. If she is to be believed, Armstrong couldn't have been actively helping the thieves. Does that help?'

'It's queer I didn't hear the story,' said Bristow, 'but there *was* a girl who said she'd been upstairs two or three times after twelve. A hot-water bottle had leaked, apparently.'

'That's the girl.'

'She simply said she'd seen and heard nothing unusual.'

'Was Armstrong generally suspected when you questioned her?'

'No.' Bristow hesitated, and stood up. 'I'll phone Horroby at Winchester, and tell him to check up on the story as soon as he can. I'll send a man to young Sharron, too.'

'You won't get past the doctor. He caught a pretty severe chill that night.'

'I can have someone standing by, anyhow.'

Bristow could not have implied more plainly that he was uneasy at the possibility of being on the wrong trail. He left soon after phoning Winchester.

Mannering decided to go to bed.

It was seven o'clock when he was awakened by the sharp ring of the telephone bell. In an instant he lifted the receiver.

'Hello, John, Flick here,' said Leverson. 'I've been offered the Glorias.'

'*What?*' Manner jerked himself up on his pillows. 'Who by?'

'A roundabout route, I'm afraid. You'd better go to a call-box, I'm not too sure that my line isn't tapped.'

Twenty minutes later Mannering reached a call-box at the end of Brook Street. Leverson would by then be waiting at one near Aldgate Station. They had found it useful to speak from call-boxes in the past, for Leverson and Mannering were equally liable to find their lines tapped during spells of unusual activity among jewel-thieves. Mannering knew the Aldgate number, and Leverson answered at once.

It appeared that Jake Rummell, a fence with whom Mannering had dealt on one occasion, was putting up the Gloria diamonds at ten thousand pounds. He had not told Leverson who he was dealing for, but had admitted that it was for a third party.

55

'What do you suggest, Flick?'

'Rummell won't talk in a job of this size,' said Leverson, 'and I think you'd better make an offer for the stones, but tell him you'll want to see them first. That might get you to the present owner, who isn't likely to let them out of his hands. You'll go disguised, of course?'

'Yes,' said Mannering, slowly. 'Thanks, Flick. Thank you very much.'

So now the die was cast, the Baron would be busy before the day was out.

Jake Rummell, in the third room of a suite of three offices above a public house in Chelsea, was a big-chinned, sharp-eyed man of thirty-five. He had a blunt, direct manner, and in the traffic in stolen gems he was known to be 'honest'. Ostensibly he was a commission agent, and he had a liking for cheap, rank-smelling cigars which occasionally gave off sparks.

Opposite him, at twelve o'clock that day, was an apparently middle-aged, portly man with greying hair. Rummell, who knew better than to ask questions of his clients, accepted him at his face value because he was a 'recommend' of Flick Leverson's.

It had taken Mannering an hour and a half to put on the disguise, and an hour to elude Detective Inspector Moss, who had been on his trail that morning. Moss was the finest shadow of the Yard; his presence proved that Bristow was not taking Mannering at all easily.

'That's right,' Rummell jerked. 'Ten thousan' smackers, on the nail, I needn't tell yer. They're cheap becos they're hot. Hottasell. You know that.'

'Indeed I do.' It was not Mannering's normal voice, but a high-pitched and querulous one. 'But I must see them, my friend. You will understand, I cannot buy—er—blind is the expression I believe.'

Rummel grinned.

'You're there in one, Mister. Wouldn't buy blind meself. You busy?'

'Er—I can spare half an hour, Mr. Rummell.'

'Quarter'll do. Just wait 'ere, an' I'll come back in fifteen minutes to the tick.'

56

He was back in fourteen minutes, slightly out of breath. 'All okey-doke, Mister. The guy'll see you. Piccadilly Circus Station, half-past three. Haymarket subway. He'll wear a red carnation in his left button-hole. Answers to Smith. If it's a deal, you don't pay him, you pay me, don't forget.'

'Naturally I shall respect that condition,' said Mannering testily.

The fence would have been flabbergasted had he known that the 'old man' was the Baron, for among the organisation of fences in London the name of the Baron ranked high.

Mannering lunched at a public house close to Sloane Square, and at half-past two, folded his paper and left the pub, his scheme already fixed. He proposed to follow the man with the red carnation, and survey the prospects of breaking into his house.

The chance of working again, of pitting his wits against police and criminal alike, the old, old thrill of the hunt gripped him. With a cause like this—not only the possibility of getting back the Glorias, but of finding the truth of the robbery—he could work with an easy conscience, and revel in it.

He reached Piccadilly Circus and strolled up and down, careful to keep to the Haymarket subway.

Three-thirty came.

He quickened his step. Was the man going to fail him, would the trail peter out?

Three minutes late.

Manner found himself both angry and dismayed. He forced back his impatience, even walking out of sight of the Haymarket subway deliberately. When he came back he saw a lean man standing idly by it, fiddling with the red carnation in his left lapel.

Mannering studied the face cheerfully.

It was glowing with health, but Mannering disliked the sharp blue eyes, the thin lips, the pinched nose. Mr Smith did not create a favourable impression.

Mannering approached with seeming diffidence. He felt the cold appraisal of the man's eyes, and knew that he was dangerous.

57

'Ah—do you, by any chance, happen to be Mr. Smith?'
'You from Rummy?'
'From Mr. Rummell, that is so.'
'Hmm.' Smith hesitated, and then shrugged his shoulders. 'All right, I've got the stuff. The Corner House suit you?'
'At your convenience, my dear sir, entirely at your convenience.'

Smith sniffed, and led the way to the Shaftesbury Avenue subway. As they approached the Corner House, the raucous voice of a newsboy startled them both.

'Big robbery—new turn. Big robbery—new turn!'

Mannering was first at the stand, and he took the paper quickly. Smith followed his example. The paragraph for which they were searching was in the Stop Press, and as Mannering read it, he experienced a sharp tingling sensation at the back of his scalp:

'Maid named Sanders found dead near *Beverley Towers* scene of big jewel robbery on Monday night. Scotland Yard officers have hurried to the scene.'

Sanders. Rose Sanders.

Mannering seemed to see Reggie's face, and then Bristow's. The girl who had seen Armstrong in his room, who could have given evidence that Armstrong had not been near the strong-room, dead and possibly murdered.

Mannering looked up, to see the glitter in Smith's sharp, suspicious eyes.

CHAPTER EIGHT

THE HOUSE AT BARNES

Mannering's clear hazel eyes were difficult to disguise; he kept them half-closed, twitching them frequently to prevent a close scrutiny; but Smith's gaze was unnerving.

'Well?' he said sharply.

Mannering took a spotted red handkerchief from his pocket and dabbed his forehead.

'Most—most disturbing,' he said in that querulous voice he had assumed. 'It makes things so much more difficult. Shall we—er—have that cup of tea?'

'Want to forget it?' Smith snapped.

'Forget our little discussion? No, indeed, these unfortunate things cannot always be avoided. One learns to accept them.' He led the way into the big hall, Smith following. It was a quiet period of the afternoon, and there were dozens of empty tables. Smith selected one in a corner, took off his hat and pushed a bony hand through his hair. The hand was unsteady, Mannering noted with grim satisfaction.

A waitress came up.

'Er—good afternoon, my dear.' Mannering beamed. 'A pot of China tea for me, and—er—my friend will have——'

'Coffee,' said Smith. 'White.'

'Coffee, yes. And some plain cakes, please.' He watched her walk off, hips swaying. No one was within earshot, but he kept his voice low. 'Well now, Mr. Smith, Rummell gave me to understand the Glorias could be bought for ten thousand. In view of the—er—strong scent, let us now say eight.'

'Ten,' said Smith decisively. 'Or nine and a half if you pay me and forget Rummell.'

'My dear sir! I really can't consider—you are not forgetting that most disquieting news? Armstrong's death, I understand, was open to doubt, but this—tacha, tacha! How careless! Eight thousand, payment against delivery, in notes of whatever denomination you like.'

'They're worth three times that,' said Smith sharply. 'But

have a look at them first, Guv'nor, and then let's talk about the price.'

He dipped his hand into his breast pocket, and drew out a case. Mannering held his breath, one hand held forward. Mr. Smith, however, did not let the case out of his grasp. He unlocked it with a small key, tilting the gems in such a way that their red-tinted glory scintillated in front of Mannering's eyes.

Twelve stones, all of them the deep pink shade which made the 'mongrels' so valuable, perfect examples of the coloured diamonds at which Fauntley had scoffed. Mannering stared at them, and through his mind flashed a dozen thoughts. Primarily amazement that Smith dared bring this string to a large public restaurant in the heart of the Metropolis, where there were more police and detectives to the square mile than in any other spot except Scotland Yard itself.

Smith did not speak for thirty seconds. He had one finger on the lid of the case, and snapped it down suddenly. Mannering heard the waitress approaching, while Smith said almost inaudibly:

'Well?'

'Yes, yes, astonishing.' Mannering said. 'I really didn't think they would be so wonderful. No, indeed! Er—but ten thousand, Mr. Smith, seeing how dangerous——' He broke off, beamed at the waitress. 'Thank you, my dear, thank you, that seems an excellent selection.'

'Nine thousand five hundred if you deal direct. Not a ha'penny less.'

'It seems——' Mannering poured out his tea, while pursing his lips. 'Rather heavy, yes, the risk is worth two thousand. However, give me ten minutes to decide, please.'

He drank and appeared to enjoy his tea. Smith let his coffee stand until it was almost cold, and then swallowed it in a few quick gulps. At the end of ten minutes he said harshly:

'Make up your mind.'

Mannering pushed the tips of his fingers together, well aware that Smith would gladly have hit him.

'Well, I think not, my friend. I have been considering the added risks of the new—er—misadventure at Beverley. I think perhaps it will be wiser for me not to touch the diamonds for a while, at any price. A thousand apologies, my dear sir.'

The thin-faced man had gone white. He stood up, swearing viciously.

'My dear sir!' Mannering teetered, 'Mr. Smith, the bill, really——'

Mr Smith was out of earshot.

Mannering signalled to the waitress, paid without waiting for change, and, hoping that Smith had taken the stairs made for the lift. He reached the ground floor as Smith barged out of the main doors.

The man who had the Glorias in his pocket was either a beginner at the game, or exceedingly subtle. His anger at the failure of the deal was alarming: now his headlong career along Coventry Street towards the Circus, without a glance behind him, suggested that he was still in the grip of overpowering rage—and that the disappointment had been very great indeed. The only apparent reason was that he badly needed the cash for the diamonds.

It was likely, of course. The more expert the cracksman the more feckless the man. Robberies were usually left until finances were in a desperate position, which accounted for much of the success of the police: jewels were too frequently on the fence-market within a few hours of their being stolen. And that the Glorias were intact, not sent to the cutters, made their early display dangerous to the thieves.

Mannering, crossing the road at the first opportunity, found it difficult to keep pace with his quarry.

He expected Smith to dive underground at the first subway, and was half-afraid that he might lose him there. But Smith went past them at the same headlong pace, finally coming to a halt at the bus-stop opposite Swan & Edgars.

Mannering beckoned a cab.

As it slowed down beside him Smith jumped on to a bus, and Mannering instructed his driver to keep the bus in sight.

The driver was good, averaging a fair distance from the bus, sometimes in front of it, sometimes dropping as much as a hundred yards behind. Occasionally Mannering could see the back of Smith's head. For nearly half an hour the chase continued, until at Hammersmith Broadway Smith alighted.

The cabby pushed the glass partition open.

'Keep after him, do I?'

'If you can, please.'

'You step out, an' I'll follow yer.'

Mannering jumped out quickly.

By now Smith had recovered his composure. He went more cautiously across Hammersmith Broadway, and stationed himself at another bus-stop.

A number 9 bus lumbered up, and Smith climbed in. Mannering found his cab running alongside him, but was uneasy in his mind. Did Smith suspect he was being followed? Had that headlong rush been a clever deception?

Mannering sat back in a corner, and began to work fast. He removed the supplementary moustache with the help of a small bottle of spirit, and then cleaned out the cleverly dyed grey hair, at the back and sides of his head. Next he worked quickly at the thin rubber covering of his teeth. From his pocket he took a featherweight mackintosh. Discarding his velvet-collared coat he donned the other. By the time the bus had reached Hammersmith bridge the passenger was unrecognisable as the portly gentleman who had protested at being left to pay the Corner House bill.

Castelnau, Barnes, was familiar to Mannering. It was a wide road, with large detached houses on either side, one of the most residential thoroughfares in South-west London. Smith alighted halfway along it.

Mannering looked out of the side window, but Smith did not turn back. He reached one of the houses, easily identifiable by a fine cypress hedge, and hurried along the carriage-way. Mannering tapped on the glass, and the cab slowed down, enabling him to see that Smith did not stand long outside the front door.

'That what yer want?' asked the cabby, turning round. 'I—*Gawd*!' His face, fat and cheerful, twisted into an expression of dismay. ''Ere, who the hell are you?'

'You've done well,' said Mannering, and his voice was identifiable if his face was not, as he took two pound notes from his pocket. 'Pull into the other side of the road, and then drive across the bridge and wait for me there.' He winked. 'A divorce job.'

'Strewth!' said the Cabby. 'You ought to be at the Yard, not a private dick.'

Mannering walked along Castelnau with long, springy strides, until he was within easy distance of the house with the cypress hedge.

It stood no more than thirty yards from the pavement, but the hedge hid most of the ground-floor windows. It was four-storied, Mannering saw, newly-painted, and giving evidence of prosperity. A large iron gateway led to the garage at the side of the house. It had no name, but was numbered 31x.

Striding past, he felt a considerable satisfaction. He reached a small row of shops, including a Post Office, where he borrowed a street directory at the counter. A few minutes searching enabled him to learn that 31x Castelnau, was owned or tenanted by a Mr. Cornelius Gillison.

At the far end of the Bridge he found the cabby. At half-past five he was deposited at Piccadilly Circus.

Gillison was dark, broad-shouldered and stocky, with a pleasant voice which did not appear to be giving Smith much pleasure at the moment.

'So you failed to get any particulars of the man, you showed him the stones, and when he wouldn't buy you rushed away, letting him follow you as far as the Circus, and then losing sight of him. Not,' added Gillison bitingly, 'a brilliant morning's work, Smith.'

'He wasn't a dick, I'll swear to that,' muttered Smith.

'You're not in a position to swear to anything,' retorted Gillison coldly. In the clear light of the room, Smith's pale angularity showed up in marked contrast to Gillison's swarthy face and black hair. Yet about Gillison there was, in spite of the near-black eyes, an impression of disguise, of stageyness.

'You are sure you weren't followed?'

'I'll lay me shirt on it,' Smith said.

'In view of your recent efforts,' Gillison murmured silkily, 'your shirt would hardly confirm your reliability to me. What made you lose your head?'

63

Smith licked his lips.

'I thought it was all over bar the shouting—and I could do with the five hundred,' he added.

Gillison's eyes were veiled.

'That is another matter I must discuss with you. I pay you a fair, weekly wage, plus commission, yet you are always short of money. I'm told you gamble. Is that true?'

'I 'ave a little flutter now and then, but that's all.'

'I don't want excuses. Look——' Gillison pointed to the other's coat-sleeve. 'Frayed edges, patched shirts. You have received over a thousand pounds from me this year, and you dress like a tramp. You've only got to start drinking, my friend, and I shall no longer require your services. As it is, you will be relegated. All right, get out.'

Smith drew a deep breath.

''Alf a mo'. I need a pony quick, before the week's out.'

Gillison stared into those light grey, desperate eyes, then he unlocked a drawer and pulled out four five-pound notes, and five ones. He pushed them across his desk.

'I shall deduct it from your next commission, of course.'

'Okay, Boss!' Smith was breathing hard, as though after a long and hazardous journey. 'So long.'

As his sharp footfalls echoed down the stairs, Gillison left his study—which was on the third floor—for his bedroom on the second. Here, consulting a small notebook taken from his waistcoat pocket, he opened a wall safe, the combination of which was altered daily. He placed the Glorias in the safe, alongside several other cases, relocked the safe, and left the room.

An hour afterwards he was sitting opposite Matthew Mendleson; and no one who saw them together could have doubted that they were close relatives.

Mannering had no appointment for dinner, and he preferred to keep away from Fay until he had some definite news. Moreover he was to be busy that night, and he needed as much time as possible to prepare. Half of his preparations were complete: from Piccadilly he had gone to Fuller Mansions, a block of service flats in Park Lane, and rented a flat. He had paid a month's rent in advance, and given his name as Moore. Before the deal he had worked on his rub-

64

ber teeth covering, confident that the porter and clerk who attended him would never be able to identify him with John Mannering.

From the Piccadilly cloakroom he had collected three cases and left them at Park Lane. It was nearly seven o'clock before he had finished and, with a copy of all three evening papers, he went to Brook Street. Over a meal sent up from the restaurant he read a more detailed account of the death of Rose Sanders.

The girl's body had been discovered in a deep, fast-running stream on the borders of the estate. It had been found that morning, just before mid-day, after the girl had been missing all night. She had last been seen at a dance in Beverley where, with most of the *Towers* servants, she had been from eight until twelve.

No one had thought anything odd about Rose Sanders leaving the hall with a stranger. Rose, it appeared, had been flighty, frequently changing her cavaliers. The description of the man who had left the village hall with her varied so much as to be useless.

Mannering was convinced, now, that Armstrong had been pushed over the quarry deliberately. The subsequent murder of the girl who might have helped to clear him made that virtually certain.

Mannering planned to be at Park Lane at nine o'clock, and to leave there disguised and with his kit, at half-past ten. An hour to get to Barnes, by devious routes, and then a start on the burglary soon after the last light went out.

He lay full-length on his bed after dinner, knowing that it might be twelve hours or more before he had another chance to rest. But his nap was disturbed by the sharp ring of the front door bell.

He straightened his tie, smoothed his hair, and opened the door, half-prepared to find Bristow. Instead he saw Errol, Sharron's dismissed watchman.

Errol still had the stamp of the Yard about him. He had been a sergeant for twenty years, and a sergeant's pension was not a large one. Mannering had an idea what he wanted.

'Hallo, Errol, come in.'

'Thanks, sir.' Worried brown eyes regarded Mannering,

as he stood awkwardly, hat in hand. 'Sorry to call so late, sir, but I thought I'd more likely find you in.'

'Sit down,' said Mannering, and stepped to his cocktail cabinet. 'A drink? Beer, or——'

'I could do with a glass of beer,' said Errol heavily. 'Very good of you to see me, Mr. Mannering. I'm that worried. I don't know what to do.'

He drank deeply, and put his tankard down with a sigh of partial satisfaction.

'I don't want to come worrying you, Mr. Mannering, only I was wondering if you could put in a word for me with his lordship. I did all I could, and 1 got knocked about for my pains, and the sack at the end of it. He knows how I'm placed; I didn't think him capable of it, I really didn't.'

Mannering's interest quickened. More evidence of the recent change in Sharron's general demeanour might be useful.

'He's very upset, of course.'

'As to that, he was upset before the robbery,' Errol said with a flash of spirit. 'We put it down to Mr. Armstrong and Miss Fay, his lordship wanting to break the engagement. But he's hardly treated me fair, sir. I've been with him for a year, I went straight from the Yard, and he promised me five years' work. My wife's got T.B., and with five youngsters, three at school, and one out of work, I needed the money. Well then,' Errol went on with an effort, 'I never expected to be kicked out without a reference!'

Mannering murmured sympathetically.

'Mind you,' Errol said with another flash of spirit, 'I'm not begging, Mr. Mannering. If his lordship will only give me a reference I'll manage to get something. I tried Mr. Mendleson, but he wouldn't even see me.'

Mannering frowned.

'No. Difficult for him, of course, he's a close friend of Lord Sharron.'

'I don't think it's that, Mr. Mannering. As a matter of fact when I was at the Yard I had some work to do with Mr. Mendleson. He hasn't forgotten it, and I don't suppose he will.'

Mannering forced himself to show no elation, but his heart was thumping. Unexpectedly the watchman was

66

bringing him word that he wanted to hear, word that Leverson was trying to get, something which might suggest that Mendleson was not all that he seemed. Bristow, of course, would know it, but Bristow was keeping a lot to himself.

He emptied the rest of the beer into Errol's tankard, offered cigarettes, and said casually:

'Nothing serious, was it?'

Errol's eyes smouldered.

'You'd be surprised, Mr. Mannering, I wouldn't trust Mendleson five minutes, him and that brother of his, Gillison, he calls himself——'

He broke off, for Mannering's hand had jerked, and beer spilled over the side of his tankard.

CHAPTER NINE

VISIT BY NIGHT

For years Mannering had schooled himself to show no surprise, no matter what startling news he received. But there were moments when the iron control broke: this was one of them. He looked down ruefully at the spilt beer.

'I was born clumsy,' he said. 'What were we talking about?'

'Mendleson,' said Errol, obviously obsessed with his story. 'It was over a bucket-shop case, Mr. Mannering, and that's when we discovered that Mendleson had a brother who calls himself Gillison. He's got a French wife, and she's a little tartar.'

'It didn't get into the Press,' said Mannering. 'Or did I miss it?'

'Oh, it didn't get that far! Mendleson covered his brother well, but they were both in it all right.'

Mannering glanced at his watch.

'What a memory you Yard chaps have! Well, I'll certainly have a word with Lord Sharron, and I may be able to help, now or a bit later. You'd no particular fear of a robbery, I suppose?'

Errol shrugged.

'I advised his lordship to get someone from Winchester, or even the Yard. It isn't safe to have valuables like that lying about, as I told him.'

'My view, too,' said Mannering ruefully. 'My own loss was pretty heavy, you know. What do you think are the chances of getting the stuff back?'

Errol shook his head.

'I wouldn't take ten to one on you seeing them again. All except the pearls will have been cut up by now. You'd be surprised——' He went into a long description of the habits of jewel-thieves and fences, all of which were equally familiar to the Baron.

Errol left at half-past eight. As the door closed behind him, Mannering's mind fastened on the one fact of great significance.

So Mendleson was Gillison's brother.

Out of the welter of uncertainties a single vital point had emerged. Everything Mendleson had done came back vividly, vague suspicions crystallised.

Mendleson, then, was the Baron's quarry, if the raid on Barnes failed.

At half-past nine, half an hour behind his schedule for the night, Mannering strolled briskly to Piccadilly Circus, and then across the Green Park. Tanker Tring was on duty, and followed at a discreet distance.

Inside again, Mannering allowed his shadow to be seen by Tring sinking into an easy-chair. That fact well established he slipped beneath the window sill and crawled to his bedroom. Here he donned a black, lightweight mackintosh, and went out, this time through the door leading to the fire-escape.

No lights showed clearly enough to reveal him to any watcher, but it was possible that the police were at the back of the building as well as the front. Quietly, he went across the small courtyard to the tradesmen's entrance. Without a sound he opened it, and stepped into the narrow alleyway beyond.

There was no sound, no sign of a watcher.

The dark coat and gloves merged in the blackness. For once there was no moon, and a high wind helped to deaden all sound of his movements. Immediately opposite him was a door to the next block's domestic entrance, and Mannering stepped quickly to it.

He went through.

As he did so he saw the outline of a man's head and shoulders, and he knew that Bristow was taking every precaution to prevent the Baron working undetected. Mannering kept the gate open, and watched that lone, cold figure. The man did not move for twenty seconds, and when he did it was with the slow, ponderous footsteps of the beat-policeman turned plain-clothes man. He made two turns along the alley before Mannering was satisfied he had noticed nothing.

Mannering stepped across the second courtyard, hurrying along the passage. He had to pass the end of Brook Street to get to Piccadilly, and he saw Tring moving up and down, flapping his arms.

He taxied to the end of Park Lane, and then walked to Fuller Mansions, keeping his head down and his chin tucked into his collar—reasonable enough on a night of such piercing cold. The night-porter at the mansions grunted goodnight. Mannering hurried upstairs.

His disguise took him an hour.

Everything was done slowly, carefully. Until that day, it was some months since he had used a disguise, and he knew the danger of the slightest flaw. In front of the dressing-table glass his complexion changed from dark tan to a muddy pallor, his teeth, with the rubber covering, turned from white to yellow, his eyebrows grew thicker.

He used a white dye, easily removed with spirit, for his hair, and added a close-cropped moustache, flecked with grey. His face finished, he leaned back and studied the effect.

Satisfied, he dressed quickly, in evening dress made by an East End tailor. The clothes gave his shoulders an added slope, making him look leaner and lending him the appearance of a man dressed to kill.

Light shoes, soled and heeled with rubber, completed the outfit.

About his waist he fastened a tool-kit, containing all the implements he was likely to need, four small sticks of dynamite, two of gelignite, some stout celluloid and a folding jemmy made of high-tensile steel.

In his tail pockets he carried a small gas-pistol, loaded with ether gas, a wash-leather bag with a chloroform-soaked pad, a dark blue silk scarf and a pair of cotton gloves.

The Baron was ready.

He felt the old thrill as he went out of the room locking the door carefully behind him, the love of the chase, the familiar zest for adventure, for danger. The need for quick-wittedness, for making not a single mistake nor losing a precious moment, was with it. The years rolled by, he knew that at heart the Baron would never be finished, no matter how rigidly Mannering fought against him.

The porter was reading in the small office, and did not glance up. Mannering looked at his watch; although it was already half-past eleven, he decided not to take a cab. Changing buses at Hammersmith, he alighted near the cypress hedge.

Castelnau was almost deserted.

A few private cars, and no more than three pedestrians, were in sight. There was no sign of a policeman.

A few lights gleamed from the houses, but none from 31x.

He had been given no opportunity of reconnoitring the house of Cornelius Gillison, but that did not perturb him. As he stepped boldly into the house drive next to 31x and then across a small garden patch towards the cypress hedge, his pulse beat fast.

He was the Baron, about to break in.

The hedge stopped alongside the house, and there was a low wall dividing the two gardens. Lights on the back of the house next to 31x were shining, but Gillison's house was in darness, back and front.

It was half-past twelve when Mannering reached the back door. A piercing wind was blowing almost at gale strength. Mannering thrust his hands in his pockets, to lessen the stiffness of cold. Warmed, he tied the scarf about

70

his face.

Next door the light went out.

A bus rumbled by, and another gust of wind swept down, creating a dozen noises. It had the advantage of enabling Mannering to work unheard, though it also prevented him hearing anything that might portend danger.

His senses alert, he shone a pencil beam on the lock of the back door. It looked easy enough, but the door would probably be bolted.

He took skeleton keys from his pocket, and metal clicked on metal.

It seemed an age, but actually only thirty seconds passed before the lock clicked back. Mannering tried the handle, and pushed, but the door did not move.

He shone the torch again, spotting the gap between door and jamb. From his tool-kit he took a thin file, and pushed it through. He felt something give, knew that it was a felt runner to keep out draughts. The reverse edge of the file, knife sharp, pierced the felt and, very slowly, the Baron cut at it.

As the file reached the top he waited tensely.

The blade touched the bolt.

He shone the torch again, revealing the slit felt, and the shining steel of a bolt a quarter of an inch thick. There was a thin wire running across it. His heart leapt. Any attempt to draw it with the wire there would have raised the alarm. Even to touch it might do so.

To work at it effectively the Baron needed something to stand on. He drew away carefully, and went alongside the house as the heavy tread of a patrol policeman came clearly. Mannering waited until the man passed, his helmet showing above the cypress hedge. A car hummed by

Shining the torch towards the ground, Mannering found what he wanted—a thick log of wood, used for chopping sticks. He lifted it to the back porch, found that it was steady beneath his weight, and then took a pair of thin-mawed wire-cutters from his pocket.

It was a crucial moment.

A first-class wiring system would react at a touch; the less effective type needed pulling or jerking. He shone the light with his left hand, and opened the maws of the cutters,

71

to cut against the bolt.

The strong-levered handles pressed.

The maws bit into the wire, and the Baron's pulse was racing, there was a loud humming in his ears. But he heard no jangling of bells.

The wire snapped.

There was a lull in the wind, and he heard the ends fall against the sides of the door. Breathlessly he waited, forcing himself to keep quiet for three minutes. There was no sound; the traffic had practically ceased, only in the distance could he hear a car engine.

Satisfied, he gripped the bolt between the maws of the cutter, and began to slide it slowly back. Two minutes of delicate handling, and the end of the bolt came in sight. He drew a deep breath as he stepped off the log, lifting it away before he started work on the second bolt.

In another three minutes that too was forced back.

As he tried the handle again he felt a stab of apprehension, the inevitable moment of nervousness. He opened the door.

Darkness and silence met him.

He stepped through, closing it gently behind him. For the first time he dared to move the beam of light so that he could see properly about the room. It was large, barely furnished, and modern. In a grey-enamelled range the embers of a fire glowed red.

Mannering stepped to it, seeing that practically all the coal had burned out, assuming that the staff had retired for at least an hour.

The far door was closed but not locked, and a narrow passage lay beyond.

He went along it carefully, reaching the front hall.

The risk of failing to check the servants had been unavoidable. A snap raid at a time when the Kallinovs were likely to be on the premises had been necessary. He wanted the gems for anything that would give him a direct line between Gillison and the theft, and between Gillison and Mendleson in the same connection.

It was difficult to believe that Gillison would keep many valuables here by night; he must have known his precautions would keep out only second-rate cracksmen.

The Baron looked into the four downstairs rooms, finding them empty. Before he went upstairs he located the battery box of the telephone, and pulled out and cut one of the wires.

There would be no S.O.S. sent from the house that night.

He went quickly but quietly up the carpeted stairs, hearing no sounds.

Pausing at the first landing he tried the handle of the door nearest to him. As it turned, he heard the heavy breathing of a man. An arc lamp outside shone into the room, and as the seconds passed he could distinguish the bed with its rumpled bedclothes.

The man lying there was asleep, his mouth open. The Baron saw who it was; and for a moment he stood unmoving, his breath coming fast.

Mendleson *was* here.

The discovery would have been stupefying but for the information he had received from Errol; slowly he drew his gas-pistol from his pocket.

Mendleson made no move.

The single charge—one of three in the pistol—would keep him unconscious for five minutes, long enough for Mannering to explore the room.

Accustomed to the light now, he could see everything clearly. He lifted pictures from the walls, careful to make no sound, but found no wall-safe. The drawers of dressing-table, chest and wardrobe all opened, some squeaking a little and making him pause. They yielded nothing.

So he had to find another room, and Mendleson must be kept quiet for twenty minutes or more. He slipped his hand into his pocket for the chloroform pad, drew it out——

And then the light came on.

It came with a devastating suddenness that sent a chill of fear through him. He turned sharply, but he knew in a moment that he was cornered; for the girl who stood there had a gun in her hand.

She was tall and thin, a loose dressing-gown flung over silk pyjamas. Mannering did not see the beauty of her face, only the danger she threatened.

CHAPTER TEN

THE FEMALE OF THE SPECIES

The future loomed, an abyss, in front of him. If he lost, if
the police were called and he was captured, it meant the
end of Mannering as well as the Baron. No explanation of
motives would help him. Knowing this, he would have been
prepared to tackle a man. That it was a woman made it
more difficult.

To the woman with the gun he was nothing but a
shadowy figure holding a chloroform pad. Eyes, mouth,
nose and chin were covered. Behind him Mendleson
breathed sonorously.

Why didn't she call for help?

Why did she step towards him, her tread cat-like? There
was a feline grace in that slim body, and he saw hat her
eyes were green. He stepped back a pace, and as he moved
she spoke, her voice low but sharp.

'Do not move!'

There was nothing in her accent to suggest that she was
foreign, unless it was too clear an intonation: 'Do not' instead of 'don't'; but he took it for granted that she was
Gillison's daughter, and remembered that his wife was
French. He felt easier now that he was out of the line of the
window, knowing that their shadows could not be seen
from the street. Behind her the door was open. He was
wondering whether the others had been aroused, how heavy
the odds would be when he made his effort. Already he was
overcoming the repugnance of tackling the woman as he
waited for the inevitable moment when her alertness would
relax.

He kept still, and she spoke again.

'Who are you?'

Very simple and straightforward; almost childish, but
she did not look like a child. She was playing for time, of
course, until help came. Mannering's muscles tensed.

'I'm called many things——'

'Your name, or I shall shoot you.'

74

She moved the gun forward a fraction of an inch. She was no more than three yards from him, and a single movement would be enough to knock the gun out of her hand. But she would shoot, he sensed that; and there was the double danger of the explosion and of being wounded. And she had to be induced to come nearer.

'My name isn't important,' he mumbled. 'I'll pay you——'

As he expected she came a step nearer. Speaking in the same clear but soft voice, she said:

'Take off the mask.'

It was the moment he had been waiting, almost praying for. He lifted his hands to his mask, untied it slowly, and then as he pulled it away from his face he flung it at her. She gasped at the unexpected move, giving him time to grip her wrist in a paralysing clasp. It was child's play to get the gun away with his left hand, and he was glad now that it had been a woman, more glad that there had been no need to hurt her.

Why hadn't she screamed?

'Close the door, very quietly,' he said, and the gun in his hand was a sufficient threat to make her obey. One moment afraid, facing what seemed hopeless odds, the next on top of the world: a hundred times the Baron had known that quick transition, it was all part of the desperate game.

He took the chloroform pad out of its bag with his left hand, stepped backwards and, still training the gun on her, dropped the pad over Mendleson's mouth. He left it for sixty seconds, then withdrew it. All the time the girl had watched, her breast heaving convulsively. Mannering knew that she was desperately afraid, and he believed he knew the reason.

'What—what have you done to him?'

'Sent him to sleep for a while,' the Baron assured her, lightly.

Her eyes did not look away from his.

'So you're Yvonne Gillison?'

She nodded.

'How many others are in the house?'

The sharpness and the menace in his voice persuaded her. Her mother was away, she said, Gillison slept in the

75

next room, and she had come from a room opposite. There were three women servants, and a manservant named Grant.

All the time the unreality of the situation hovered about the Baron like a cloak: it was all too good to be true, there was something about her that he did not understand. A single cry, when she had first seen him, would have aroused both her father and the butler. Instead she had raised no alarm.

The question kept echoing through his mind: *why, why, why?* But he worked on the facts, taking what advantage he could from them.

How old was she? He had thought her near thirty when he had first seen her: now he wondered whether she was out of her teens. There was the indefinable look of the Parisienne about her.

'Where does your father keep his valuables?'

'In the safe.'

'What room?'

'His bedroom.'

'Is it a combination safe?'

'Yes—you turn the knob.' Something of her fear had dropped away, as though when the tables had first been turned she had been afraid that he would shoot her. 'What is it you want, why are you here?'

'Shall we say that I would like to add some jewels to my little collection?' asked the Baron softly.

'Which one are you?'

The question came as though she had been pondering it all the time. *'Which one are you?'* The implications made the Baron's lips tighten, but the need for working quickly was pressing, he wanted to lose no time.

'You have never been here before,' she went on slowly. 'Of that I am sure. Smith I could understand. Or Mervin, or Rogerson, but you are a stranger.'

'This is interesting,' said the Baron, his voice hardening, 'but I haven't time to listen to it Yvonne!' She jerked her head up,.and the fear came back. 'Do—as—I—tell—you!'

She nodded, her eyes feverishly bright.

Mendleson would be unconscious for at least a quarter of an hour, and it was unlikely now that there would be an alarm. A quarter of an hour might be enough, provided he could find the combination of the safe.'

'Open your father's door, and make no sound.'

She obeyed, turning the handle as softly as the Baron would have done. He was surprised when the door opened, and again misgivings filled him. Gillison was not likely to keep valuable gems in a room which was not locked. But it solved his first problem: he had been puzzling a way to open the door without giving the girl a chance to break away.

'Step into the room, very quietly.'

His whisper could hardly have reached her ears, but she went forward. The light shining from Mendleson's room illuminated Gillison's, and he could see the large mahogany furniture, the two beds, one neat and made-up the other with Gillison sleeping—as Mendleson had been—on his back. Even in the vague light the likeness between the two men was apparent.

The window opened on to the back garden. Through it he could see a light in a house perhaps three hundred yards away, but there was no fear of being overlooked.

She watched him, wide-eyed, as he moved towards the occupied bed. Her unnatural obedience, all lack of anger, worried him. But he had to take it on its face value for a while.

She gasped as he pressed the gas-pistol into action. Gillison breathed heavily, and settled down on his pillow, a sure sign that the gas had taken effect. Mannering followed with the chloroform. He had only the servants to worry about now, and there seemed no reason why they should be disturbed.

Gillison had made no attempt to hide the safe. It was between the two beds, the metal reflecting the subdued light. He was fast approaching the moment when he would have to send the girl to sleep for a while: a charge of ether gas would be enough, she was not likely to have more than a headache after it. But he wished he could understand her unnatural calm. It was all too good to be true, some sub-conscious sense carried a premonition of danger which he could not understand. He forced it away.

'Do you know the combination?'

77

'He keeps it in his wallet. Under his pillow.'

Fantastic. Everything was being done for him. He forgot that in any case he would have searched under the pillow after putting Gillison to sleep, that her arrival had in fact slowed his progress. Was she *willing* to help him? Or was there a trick?

'Get the wallet, find the combination, and put it on the dressing-table.'

White hands with polished nails moved towards the pillow. They made no sound. From a small notebook in the wallet the girl tore a page and put it on the dressing-table obediently.

'It is today's,' she said. 'He alters it each night.'

'Thanks. Now——'

Something in her expression startled him. Her lips opened, he was prepared for a scream, and he thrust the automatic forward. But when she spoke her voice was pitched on a low key. But it was vibrant with an under-current of passion.

'The money, let me have the money! I must get away, understand that, I must get away! You can have everything else, everything, but get me away!'

So that was it, and that explained her fear, her whole behaviour. She was frightened of her father, or of the house, and she wanted his help to escape. He said slowly:

'We'll see. Can you open the safe?'

'Yes, yes!' She clutched the paper and read it, muttering the numbers aloud. Her hands seemed to fly as she twisted the knob this way and that. The tumbrils clicked clearly through a silence otherwise broken only by her quick breathing.

A final click, and she pulled the door open, then swung round on him fiercely.

'A hundred pounds, that will be enough, *please*!'

'I think I can promise you that,' said the Baron. His mind was in a whirl. He had met some strange developments before, but never the daughter of a victim who helped him willingly, and then pleaded for his help. He decided to take a chance on her genuineness. Laying the gun on the dressing-table within easy reach of his hand he took a sheaf of notes from the safe, and then three jewel-cases. His hands

78

were steady as he opened the first case, but his breath was coming quickly. All the time he felt the gaze of the girl towards the wad of notes on the bed, near Gillison's arm.

The clasp opened easily.

He looked at the necklace inside, and his first thought was of disappointment: they were not the Glorias, nor were they part of the Kallinovs. Again a warning reared up in his mind, a premonition that things were not as they seemed. He stared down at the diamonds: to a casual eye they would have been convincing, but he suspected they were paste.

He looked more closely.

Paste, without doubt. His lips tightened, and he opened the second case. It was empty. The third had pearls, so obviously cultured that he spared them only a quick glance, and then looked sharply at the girl.

'Does he keep stuff anywhere else?'

'There—there in his study.'

'Another safe?'

'No. His desk.'

It was hardly likely that Gillison would keep the real valuables in a desk when the safe was available, and yet he knew Smith had brought the Glorias here. Of course, Gillison might have sent or taken them somewhere else, but the Baron could not avoid the feeling that this visit was a futile one, that it would end in frustration if not in disaster.

Yvonne's green eyes were uncanny in their appeal.

'We'll go down,' he said. 'Is it on the ground floor?'

'No, no, above! They are his offices, above them the servants——'

'Let's move,' snapped the Baron.

They had spent seven minutes in the room: Gillison and Mendleson were good for another seven.

They reached the study on the third floor.

Only one drawer was locked, and that not with a patent. The girl watched Mannering slip his skeleton key in, twist dexterously for ten seconds, and heard the lock click back. The drawer slid open. Inside was a cash box: but it contained less than thirty pounds in banknotes, and a small bag of silver. There was nothing else of importance.

How much longer dared he stay?

79

The vague fear that something was wrong kept worrying him. What explained it? It was not the girl, it was nothing that had happened here. He went through the conversation with Errol, wondering if there was something in that.

His eyes sharpened.

He knew the trouble now, for the first time he was able to locate that source of apprehension, explain the undercurrent of nervousness. Errol had said that the Yard had once suspected Mendleson.

It was never safe to be at a house where the police might come.

For a moment something akin to panic seized him: he forced it back, but he'd decided to get away at once. From the upstairs safe he had taken five hundred pounds, and he had no need of it. If Yvonne's manner was a token, she would give her heart for half the amount.

Perfunctorily he looked through the other rooms. They were furnished as offices. To make a thorough search would take him an hour at least, and the warning to be away was growing more insistent.

'Downstairs,' he said briefly.

With a desperate appeal in her eyes she watched him dose the two men again, more lightly this time. As he took the pad from Gillison's face he said slowly:

'Why do you want to go?'

'That doesn't matter, I——'

'It matters a lot. Why?'

She shrugged her shoulders, her breast heaving under the stress of fierce emotion.

'I hate them all! Thieves, rogues, I hate them! And—and then they killed him, they killed *him*!'

Something clicked in Mannering's mind. He forced the thought away from him as absurd, but it returned, and he said sharply:

'Who?'

'Oh, you don't know. Bill——'

Mannering turned his face away abruptly. Even disguised he could not keep the stupefaction out of his eyes. Bill, Bill, Bill!

Armstrong!

A dozen pieces of the jigsaw seemed to drop into place.

Armstrong, a friend of Yvonne, and with an open door at *Beverley Towers*. In all likelihood a familiar of Gillison's. How easily Gillison would have been able to persuade him to do what he wanted; a bribe of a substantial reward, a knowledge of the younger man's tormented mind and need of wealth.

He said: 'Why did they kill him?'

'Oh, don't ask, don't!'

And then she stopped.

Mannering swung round towards the door.

There was no one in the passage: but the ringing had come clearly. Not the insistent burring of the telephone, but a single sharp ring, from downstairs.

The girl had turned colour, a hand went to her throat.

'The front door. Who——'

Mannering was halfway to the door, speaking as he went.

'Is there a back staircase?'

'Yes.'

'Show me quickly!' He had stuffed the money into his pockets. 'See me tomorrow at the Lyons tea-shop in Putney High Street. You know it?'

'Yes, but——'

'I'll see you get what you want then. You mustn't have it now, they might find it, suspect you. Go back to your room, pretend you've heard nothing, seen nothing.'

And then he realised that her fingerprints would be very clear on the safe. At the same moment the ringing came again, longer this time. He knew that he could not leave her to stand the racket for the theft, and he swung round at the head of the stairs.

'Go down, open the door. Tell whoever it is that the ring woke you, you've seen nothing, understand, *nothing.*'

'Yes, yes!'

'And tomorrow afternoon at four o'clock, Lyons.'

'I will be there.'

Footsteps were coming, from the stairs above them. Mannering knew from the heavy, deliberate tread, that it was the manservant; panic threatened again, but opposite Gillison's room he spoke again in an urgent whisper.

'Go down with him, keep them downstairs for five minutes, understand?'

She nodded, and went along. Mannering felt jumpy; there were so many things he wanted to do, another five minutes would have given him ample time. Now he wiped the safe, and the dressing-table clear of prints, and slipped Gillison's wallet in his pocket. There was nothing else she had handled and which might incriminate her.

He heard voices from the hall. Gillison and Mendleson were quite unconscious, there was nothing to fear from them. But who were the callers, and was it safe to get out the back way?

A moment later he heard a sharp, precise voice, and he knew that all his vague fears had been justified, knew that the sixth sense which had saved him so often from disaster had tried to warn him again, but been ignored.

For it was Bristow's voice.

CHAPTER ELEVEN

LIES OF A LADY

The Baron had come to Barnes with a conviction that even if he were caught there would be no danger from the police. Reasoning that he would not need a car for a quick escape, he had come by bus. There was a certain danger, too, in leaving a car parked in a public road after midnight, inviting, as it might, the curiosity of the patrol police.

Now he needed to put miles between himself and Barnes as quickly as he could.

There were other factors. If this was a raid, and there could be no other explanation of Bristow's call after one o'clock at night, men might be stationed at the back of the house. The girl was in almost as dangerous a position as himself. How could she explain walking past those two open doors and yet claim to have seen neither her father nor uncle unconscious? Quick wits were needed, and perhaps she had them.

He had to chance it, to stay meant inevitable disaster.

He hurried along the passage to the servants' quarters.

In his pocket was Yvonne's gun, as well as his gas-pistol. *Robbery with violence. Unlawful possession of firearms.* Indictment after indictment flashed through his mind, yet without affecting the quick decisiveness of his movements. He reached the door he had forced less than an hour before and very gently pulled it open.

He saw no one, heard nothing, not even the voices from the hall.

He went forward, towards the little pathway alongside the house. As he neared the front garden, the shadows of the cypress hedge gave him cover. He was feeling easier for, apparently, Bristow had not surrounded the house with men.

But he had left one at the front.

The Baron saw Bristow's green Morris, and the plain-clothes man standing in the carriage-way. It was impossible to climb the hedge: he had to pass the man to get outside.

Now he could hear voices. A light was coming from one of the downstairs front rooms. He could hear Yvonne's voice, and the tones told him that she was treating Bristow to a gust of Gallic temperament. It would give him five minutes or more before Bristow discovered what had happened.

The shadow of the man standing in the gateway reached almost to the Baron's feet. With the tool-kit and the money he had taken for Yvonne in his pocket, a single false move and he was finished.

Keeping close to the hedge he approached the short driveway. Slowly, fearful of jingling coins together, he withdrew a coin from his pocket. Still hidden by the shadows of the hedge, he was now ten feet from the watcher, whom he recognised as Drew, one of Bristow's most recent aides. He dared go no further.

With a deep breath Mannering tossed the coin into the air.

It seemed an age before it clinked against the pavement. At the sound, sharp and clear despite the wind, Drew turned abruptly.

83

Mannering moved.

He went fast, his final leap making no sound. Gloved hands fastened on Drew's throat, stifling a cry of warning. There was one charge left in the gas-pistol, and the Baron pressed the trigger, pointing the gun awkwardly into Drew's face. The man gasped, choked and then went limp.

Mannering waited for five seconds, and then dragged the inert body towards the hedge. But as he moved from the gateway he heard a gruff voice from the next garden.

'That you, Drew?'

So the place *was* surrounded. Mannering's heart beat a rat-tat-tat as he stepped boldly into the roadway, towards Bristow's Morris. He steadied his voice and called back in what he hoped would be taken for Drew's hushed accents, then opened the car door and slipped in. As he pulled at the self-starter and listened desperately for the engine to wake to life, he heard footsteps, and suddenly the burly form of the detective appeared in the gateway.

The engine hummed. Mannering let in the clutch and eased off the brake.

The man leapt forward, but the car swerved past him, humming along Castelnau towards Barnes. The only road the Baron knew well was that which ran over the Common, and he went all out.

There was still a fear in his mind, for in a quarter of an hour at the outside Bristow could have men at his flat, and it was impossible to get there in under half an hour. He needed a hide-out and an alibi, and he knew that the one place he might reach in time was Lorna's Chelsea studio. But Bristow knew it too—his safety depended on the time Bristow took to send men there.

As ex-Detective Sergeant Errol had told the Baron, Bristow and the police had good reason to suspect that much of Mendleson's money was not honestly earned. The moment Mendleson had been mentioned, Bristow had set inquiries afoot concerning Cornelius Gillison—a name which Gillison had taken by deed poll ten years before. But the processes of the law, as Bristow knew to his cost, were slow and cumbersome. He could not raid Gillison's house without a search warrant, nor get the Assistant Commissioner to pass a warrant without presenting him with reasonable proof of Gillison's complicity in the theft—*or* in some form of crime.

For three days Bristow had searched for an excuse. Gillison's house had been watched closely, and a man whose name appeared to be Smith had been seen to pass to and fro frequently. Neither Bristow, nor the Yard, had a record of Smith; but when he visited Jake Rummel, Bristow believed he had Gillison where he wanted; at least, he had grounds for a warrant.

Sir David Ffoulkes, one of the most human and accommodating A.C.s the Yard had known, and who chafed against the irksome regulations as much as his men, had not hesitated to give one. The indirect line between Smith, Rummel and Gillison was an excuse, good enough to use as an argument if the raid went wrong.

Bristow knew the advantage of a surprise raid and decided to execute it late at night.

The sullen-faced manservant who answered the door was insolent, and Bristow had to frighten him. Frightening him also scared the girl who had come downstairs. In Bristow's opinion she was indecently clad; he had an inherent suspicion of French women, even half-French women. In his view she had been sent downstairs while her father tried to get the stuff out of the house. Her bright, frightened eyes, her incoherent spate of words, her sudden shrieks were all convincing enough of fear. Whether she was scared by the night call, or had any reason to fear the police, Bristow did not know, but so shrill were her ejaculations that neither he nor Moss heard Mannering's scuffle with Drew, nor the start of the car. It was only faintly that he heard the ring of the front door bell.

Moss opened the door.

'Edwards! What the devil's happened?'

Bristow moved fast. He flung the door open as Edwards half-fell into the hall. His face was bruised and his eyes were heavy, as though recently unconscious. He was breathing hard, trying to find words.

'G-got—a-away! G-got——'

'Outside,' snapped Bristow, and light streamed from the hall as he rushed along the drive. When he found his car

85

gone and Drew unconscious, he had an idea of what had happened.

Moss sniffed suspiciously.

'I——' He sniffed again. 'Mr. Bristow!'

Bristow, halfway to the door and the telephone, turned about.

'What is it?'

'Gas, that's what.'

Bristow reached the unconscious Drew, and bent over him. The faint smell of ether came to him, and there flashed through his mind thought of Mannering.

'The Baron's been here! Leave him, get upstairs fast!'

They reached the hall together.

Bristow snatched up the hand-microphone. It did not immediately occur to him that it was dead, and he banged the platform up and down violently. As the realisation came to him, he saw the open battery-box, and the pulled and cut wire.

Bristow was close to losing his temper. The events of the past five minutes would have been enough in themselves, but in addition there was the possibility that Mannering had been here. But to lose his temper was to lose time. He stepped to Edwards, who was sitting in the hall chair, dazed and bewildered. He would not be fit enough to go to a telephone for ten minutes or more.

'Better go myself,' Bristow said aloud. 'There'll be one next door.'

He turned, but he had not moved towards the door when he heard his name called from upstairs. The voice of Inspector Moss, usually so quiet and self-possessed held a high-pitchèd note, as unfamiliar as it was alarming. Bristow hurried upstairs, and from the landing he called down to the manservant.

'Go to the alley at the back of the house and tell my man to come in!'

Moss was not in sight, but a light was coming from the room on the left. Bristow reached the door.

He stood quite still.

He needed every atom of self-control at that moment. He saw Moss bending over a bed, saw and recognised the unconscious Mendleson on it. At once he was sure that the

86

Baron had been there, and whatever stolen jewels there might have been on the premises would have disappeared with him. With that conviction came the hope that it was possible to stop the Baron getting to his flat. Minutes had been wasted, but the moment a call was out for Bristow's car Mannering would be finished.

'I must telephone the Yard, Moss,' Bristow said roughly. 'You stay here.'

And then the most fiendish noise of that fiendish night for Bristow, split across his ears. The girl, from the room opposite him, was screaming. The first cry came so clearly and so horribly that Bristow could not move, and Moss jumped up in alarm.

Through the half-open door Bristow could see the girl's back. Her arms were flung towards the ceiling as those heart-rending screams came out in quick succession.

Bristow pushed past her. The safe was open, empty jewel cases littered the floor, and he caught the winking of what looked like diamonds. On the bed lay Gillison, quite unconscious.

The urgent need for telephoning was swallowed up in the necessity to make sure that Gillison was alive. With the light above his head casting strange shadows over his face, the man looked ghastly. Bristow bent over him, feeling for his pulse. His own nerves were jittery, and it was some time before he made sure that the pulse was beating.

Would there be no end to the madness of that night?

For in the passage stood three women, two young and one middle-aged. The girls held pokers, and the other a broom which she gripped threateningly. Automatically he backed away.

'You stay right where you are, mister. Aggie, go and phone for the police. Go on, 'urry!'

Bristow clutched at the remnants of his self-control.

'Stay where you are!' The authority of his voice had its effect, and the girl Aggie stopped, but the women gripped their weapons no less firmly.

'I *am* a policeman,' Bristow said, wiping the sweat from his forehead and taking out his wallet. He selected a card, and the woman stretched a hand out for it suspiciously. She read it.

' 'Ow do I know it's yourn? You ain't got no uniform.'

'Eet ees so,' said Yvonne from the door, so abruptly that Bristow jumped. ' 'Ow-we-know? Answer zat!'

'You'll know all right,' Bristow said sharply. 'Another word out of any of you and I'll have you sent to the station. Is that clear?'

They were dubious, but subdued, and he believed that Yvonne Gillison's interruptions were deliberate, that she meant to stall him. But salvation, in the form of a uniformed policeman arrived before any of them spoke again. The patrolman had heard the screams, hurried into the house, seen Edwards—who had enough sense to gasp his name and say where Bristow was—and lost no time in getting upstairs.

But another five minutes passed before Bristow was able to start for the telephone, next door. He was met by a scared householder, disturbed by the screams, and was given reluctant permission to use the telephone. It was fully twenty-five minutes after the Baron had started for Chelsea before Bristow succeeded in sending the general call out for his Morris, and ordering squad cars to be sent to Mannering's Brook Street flat and Lorna Fauntley's Chelsea studio took even longer.

But by then the Chief Inspector had lost hope of getting Mannering for that night's escapade.

In an hour some sort of order had been restored at 31x Castelnau. There had been the two chloroformed men to bring round, explanations to make and hear. Gillison had his wits about him sufficiently to deny that there was anything in the house that should not be. He seemed confident enough, and as the Yard men searched his confidence seemed more and more justified.

No one admitted seeing the Baron.

When the questions were over and Bristow was sitting in the lounge with Yvonne and her father and Mendleson, one fact emerged. The girl had passed the rooms where her father and uncle had been unconscious, but had not seen them: or, Bristow thought glumly, refused to admit she had.

'I tell you, no I see nothing,' Yvonne persisted. 'I heard ze ringing, I am awake. I come down, and Grant, he comes too. At the door I find you. From then you know what happened.'

'Yes, yes,' said Bristow testily. 'But you must have realised the lights were on in the rooms, why didn't you look in?'

'I hurried to find who comes before the ring wakes everyone. My mother comes back sometimes, wit' no key. I thought it was her, can you not understand that?'

'All right,' sighed Bristow. 'That'll do.'

'I hope,' Gillison said suavely, 'that my daughter can retire now, Inspector.'

Bristow nodded. Yvonne went out, while Bristow settled back to deal with the two men. Sitting opposite him, remarkably alike, equally clever, unscrupulous, sharp-witted and acquainted with the many complexities of the law, they presented no easy task. He waited for Gillison to begin.

'After all this fuss,' Gillison said, 'I hope you can tell me what inspired your interest?'

'Certainly. A regular caller here is known to be in communication with a receiver of stolen goods.'

'Surely not the *only* reason for a raid at this time of night?' protested Gillison.

'It's enough.'

'As to that, I shall, of course, get legal opinion. What do you make of it, Matthew?'

Mendleson's dark eyes mocked the policeman's.

'Not much, I'm afraid. The visit was quite unjustified, and becomes perilously near persecution, Mr. Bristow. However, as I see it the biggest error is in allowing the thief to go. My brother appears to have lost over five hundred pounds, not to mention his wallet. And the police were actually surrounding the premises!' Mendleson sighed. 'It isn't going to make good reading in the Press, Mr. Bristow. Tell me, why did you come? I understood you were working on the *Beverley Towers* robbery.'

'That is so.'

Mendleson raised his brows.

'Indeed? I hope you don't suspect that I helped to steal my own jewels?'

Bristow said nothing.

'Well, well,' purred Gillison. 'I don't doubt I shall hear

from you again, Inspector. You will, of course, be hearing from me.'

Bristow and Moss returned to the Yard. Bristow learned that his car was still missing, that Mannering had been found at Lorna Fauntley's studio. He claimed that he was spending the night there, and had been there since twelve o'clock. Tring was sent for, and swore Mannering had not gone out through Brook Street: the man watching the back of the Brook Street flat was equally certain that he had not gone through the alleys.

'I'll see Mannering in the morning,' Bristow said tersely. He did not expect to get results from interviewing the Baron; he knew Mannering's story would have no loopholes, and that it was just another trick against the police. Wearily Bristow was driven to Gresham Street, Chelsea, where he lived.

As he stepped out he saw a stationary red rear-light outside his house.

The Baron had returned the borrowed car.

CHAPTER TWELVE

THE STUDIO

Five minutes after Mannering had reached Lorna's studio, the police had called. The disguise so laboriously built up had gone, an apparently sleepy, tousled man had answered their insistent knocking. He had raised no objection when the police-sergeant asked to search the studio. The man might be suspicious of the clothes in the wardrobe which did not seem like Mannering's, but everything incriminating was floating or sinking in the Thames, three minutes' walk from the flat.

Gresham Street, where Bristow lived, was five minutes walk in the other direction, which had enabled the Baron to leave the car and hurry to the studio. After half an hour's pottering, the police had gone, and Mannering had locked and bolted the door, then helped himself to a strong whisky-and-soda.

The first glow of triumph had passed. He was free for the time being, but the girl was in a nasty hole. Had she the wits to say nothing, to refuse to answer all questions?

Sleep seemed impossible while that question remained unanswered, but he was dead to the world when the sharp rapping came again on the door. Alert on the instant, he pulled back the bolts. A wild-eyed Bristow was standing there.

'Oh, my lord!' exlaimed Mannering. 'Not *again*!'

'You've carried the joke too far, Mannering!'

'Joke?' Mannering guessed that Bristow had had a completely unsuccessful evening, that he was tired out, that in all likelihood he had called so soon because of the car outside his house. He felt sorry for the policeman, but his own policy was clear. 'I don't think much of a joke calling me out of bed twice in the same night, and I'm tired of it. Have you recovered the Glorias?'

'You know damned well I haven't, you've got them yourself.'

Mannering's voice was low and biting.

'So it's the old game? The police are baffled and they try to blame me or the Baron. Bristow, I'm not having men follow me about as they've been doing for the past three days. It's got to finish.'

Bristow gathered about him the last remnants of self-control.

'Then tell me: where have you been tonight?'

'Here.'

'You were at your flat at eleven o'clock.'

'And left at half-past.'

'You weren't seen to leave.'

Mannering shrugged.

'What time did you get here?'

'Midnight, as near as dammit.'

'Why did you come?'

Mannering dropped his sharp manner, knowing that Bristow was not seriously hoping to get past his guard.

91

'Well, Bill, if you must know the truth I was annoyed at finding Tring peeping at me from behind every lamp-post. I decided to teach him a lesson. I didn't fancy a hotel, so I came here. It's time you had a drink.' He poured out a generous tot of whisky.

Bristow took it, swallowed it at a stretch and then unexpectedly laughed. That saving grace of his, a capacity to laugh when the joke was against himself, made Mannering warm to the man.

'All right, drat you, but I'll get you soon. You *may* be after your own jewels, but you've got to keep inside the law. Once and for all—will you stop it?'

'The only time I went outside the law,' said Mannering easily, 'was when I did thirty-two miles an hour in a thirty area, but no one saw me. You look tired, Bill, what's the matter?'

In Bristow, two sides warred. He knew that Mannering had been to Barnes, and was equally certain that he would not be able to prove it. He was inclined to believe that Mannering's motive had been to regain his lost jewels, and perhaps those of the other four victims. Had he been convinced that was all, he would have given him his head, for Mannering's connection among fences was far more likely to yield results than the ordinary routine of the police.

But if the Baron found Sharron's jewels, as well as the others, would they ever be returned?

Bristow doubted it. He dared strike no bargains with the nonchalant man in front of him, he had to work against the Baron as well as the thieves at Beverley. Now that the whisky had done its work he realised the futility of this visit to Mannering, who was never without an answer, never off his guard.

'If you don't know what's the matter, Mannering, look in the papers in the morning. By the way, what did you think of the girl?'

'What girl?'

'Oh well,' said Bristow. The trick question, so often successful, was useless against Mannering. 'If you won't take a warning, I can't help you.'

'I'll have to try to help myself,' murmured Mannering, and as Bristow turned to the door, he said quietly: 'Bill, did I read something about a girl found murdered at Beverley?'

Bristow's face grew hard.

'Yes. Of course, you——' he hesitated.

'Made you curious about her,' said the Baron. 'I've been thinking this way, Bill. Young Sharron told me her story, but at secondhand it's hardly evidence. Firsthand, from Rose Sanders, it might have been evidence for Armstrong's defence. Oh, I know he won't be standing in the dock, but that's no reason why he shouldn't be proved innocent—if he was.'

There was a grimness about Mannering's eyes which surprised Bristow, although it should not have done. In the past he had known the Baron go into action with no greater cause than to prove a man's innocence, when he had had the same end in view as Bristow.

Was he making Armstrong's complicity a cause?

'Of course not,' Bristow said. 'But I think Armstrong was a party to the theft, even if in a small way.'

'But Armstrong died, and he can't talk. The girl died, and she can't talk. Significant, don't you think? I wonder if there isn't something deeper behind it, something you haven't seen yet, and I'm groping for.'

Bristow shrugged.

'We'll find it eventually and there's no need at all for you to interfere. You're risking your own safety for something that doesn't directly concern you, Mannering. Why must you do it?'

For once the Baron did not evade the question.

'Bill,' he said, 'I've taken a fancy to Fay Sharron, and a dislike to her parents. Incidentally, I'm not impressed by Matthew Mendleson.'

'You know where Mendleson was tonight?'

'I haven't a notion.'

'Who are you fooling?' snapped Bristow. 'I'm going.'

As the door closed behind his visitor, Mannering stared thoughtfully at it for some minutes, and then with a yawn he went back to bed, and slept.

Something soft against his cheek awakened him.

He was alert on the instant, forcing his breathing to keep steady, tensing the muscles of his arms in readiness for a spring. When he opened his eyes it was with a cry of relief, as they rested on Lorna.

As she settled a tray of morning tea at his side, he noted the hint of apprehension in her fine eyes.

For a time she chatted affectionately of nothing in particular, then she said carefully:

'You were at Gillison's house last night, darling, and whoever knows Mannering as the Baron might not be pleased about it.'

'It's a point,' admitted the Baron as carefully. 'But I'm truly not worrying. How did you know I'd been to Barnes?'

Lorna glanced at a pile of papers behind her. 'Did you get anything worth getting?'

He related the story briefly, with the easy, almost flippant way she knew so well. Through the adventure of the night she lived almost as vividly as the Baron, but it was Reggie Sharron's story and the murder of the maid that worried her most. Mannering could see that she was wishing she had not urged him to find the truth about Armstrong, but that would pass, she would soon be as anxious as he to justify Fay's belief in the man.

And the clear-cut case of murder now made it far more urgent.

'So you think it was Mendleson and Gillison?'

'It's looking that way,' said the Baron. 'But I'm interested in Sharron, too. He refused to have a police guard that night although I advised it strongly, and so did Errol, the watchman. Errol takes the charitable view, although he's reason enough to be vindictive against Sharron.'

'The charitable view?'

'That Sharron's been worried by the Fay–Armstrong engagement, and is a little off his balance because of it.'

Lorna poured out more tea as she said decisively:

'The police seem to agree that Mendleson's the man, and you've reached the same conclusion. Armstrong is already a party to it, and now if you start bringing Sharron in——'

Mannering lifted a hand.

'Easy, angel! Armstrong's case is still "not proven".'

'I don't think anyone, Fay included, would agree with you over that,' said Lorna as decisively as before. 'But she does want to know what forced him to do it, she just doesn't believe it was for the sake of the money. No, John. Sharron

94

had good cause to be worried, you can't reasonably suspect him.'

'As to that, you may be right,' said the Baron evasively. 'What's the time?'

'Nearly eleven.'

'As late as that? Angel, start cooking my breakfast, and I'll be ready in ten minutes.'

Using the shaving kit that he kept at the studio, and dressing in a lounge suit also there for emergency, he was actually ready in a quarter of an hour. Lorna had grilled bacon and tomatoes, and he set to hungrily while she glanced through the London papers.

The burglary at Castelnau had been starred, and talk of the Baron was rampant again.

'Feeling proud of yourself?' Lorna asked, as she picked up another of the papers.

'No, darling, proud of you and your way with tomatoes. Who taught you to cook?'

'Who taught the Baron to pick locks?' demanded Lorna.

It was fifteen minutes before they left the studio. They walked to Portland Place, but Mannering did not go in, while at his flat his first task was to telephone Gregory.

'Young Sharron's about as well as you can expect,' Gregory said gruffly, 'but why the devil did you have to tell the police about it, Mannering? There's a jackanapes here all the time, and the passage is filled with blasted kids peeking at him.'

'It had to be done,' said Mannering. 'When will he be able to talk rationally?'

'In forty-eight hours—*if* he has enough rest,' grunted the doctor.

So Reggie was off the list of visitors for another two days. Mannering felt impatient, wondered whether the peer's son had told all of his story. He could not erase his impression that it was a deeper business even than the police suspected.

And, too, he was beginning to wonder whether Bristow had gone to raid Gillison, or gone to try to find the Baron.

No one had known of his intended visit: but someone might have followed him, might have learned of the flat in Park Lane. It was a disquieting thought, and he had to fight against a temptation to ask Bristow direct questions.

He was more disturbed when, just after one-thirty, he left the flat to find no policeman watching him.

Bristow had every reason for strengthening the guard, none for cancelling it. Mannering was afraid of a trick, and he walked for half an hour about Regent Street and Piccadilly, watching carefully for a sign of a shadow. He saw no one, discovered nothing that encouraged his vague fears.

He took a taxi to Fuller Mansions, and waited on the opposite side of the Lane for a few minutes before going into th block. He saw no one he knew, was certain he was not followed. But the uneasiness remained.

Altering his face from Mannering's to Moore's was a quicker business this time, and before three o'clock he slipped out of the back entrance of the Mansions. Yvonne would not recognise him, for he had made vital alterations to his disguise of the night before, but it would not be difficult to prove to her that it was the Baron. In his pockets were five hundred pounds: the original notes taken from Gillison's safe were floating in the Thames, but Mannering meant to keep his word to Yvonne.

Unless he did she would not be likely to talk, and he knew there was good reason to believe she could explain many things. He was intrigued at the fact that young Yvonne Gillison and Bill Armstrong had been in any way associated. He had not told Lorna of that: it would strengthen the case against Armstrong, and he wanted her to believe in the man for the time being.

At four o'clock, confident that no one had followed him, he stepped into the Lyons tea-shop in Putney High Street.

He selected a small table near the door, and looked about him. Less than twenty people were drinking tea or eating buns. He saw Yvonne at once, but before talking to her he wanted to weigh up the opposition.

It was considerable, for it was Tanker Tring.

Mannering's eyes narrowed, but he felt more reassured. Bristow had taken the guard off Mannering to put it on the girl, and that move did the Chief Inspector credit. Mannering knew that Bristow was shrewd, but he had hardly expected him to suspect that the Baron might meet Yvonne again. It meant, of course, that Yvonne had given cause for suspicion on the previous night.

He felt a little pulse in his right temple ticking with anxiety. It he went to the girl and introduced himself to her, Tring *might* act. Bristow had set this trap with his customary care.

Mannering signalled a waitress. He had already ordered tea; and this time he suggested cream buns, going on to say pleasantly:

'The young lady in the corner—has she yet had her bill?'

'No, sir.' The waitress's face was expressionless.

'Can you arrange for a little note to be sent to her, when the bill is delivered?' He offered a florin, and the waitress nodded as she took it. Mannering scribbled on a page from his notebook, while Tring occupied himself by drinking tea and ostentatiously studying the sports news.

Mannering waited long enough to see Yvonne take the note. His opinion of the girl rose: she accepted it as though it were nothing unusual, and certainly there was no need for Tring to suspect that as well as her bill she had the brief instructions which Mannering had written.

Take a bus to the top of Putney Hill. Wait for me there.

CHAPTER THIRTEEN

YVONNE

To walk to the nearest garage, hire a small saloon car and to reach the top of Putney Hill, took the Baron twenty minutes. Yvonne was waiting, standing near the bus-stop, and Tanker Tring was fifty yards away from her, on the same side of the road. Mannering watched closely, and saw no car standing near by. Tring, then, was on foot. It made the Baron's task easier.

He no longer felt worried. Bristow's trick was obvious, and it was fighting the unexpected that perturbed the Baron. He drew up sharply in front of Yvonne. In the driving mirror he saw Tring hurrying forward, but the sergeant was thirty yards away.

Yvonne looked startled.

'In, quickly,' snapped the Baron, and his voice was unmistakable. She acted without a moment's hesitation; as Mannering opened the door she slipped next to him, and the car started off again.

Tring ran the last few yards desperately, but was still well behind when they moved. Mannering could imagine the man's quandary. Whether to use his whistle and try to get the car stopped, or to admit that Yvonne had slipped him.

Mannering laughed softly. At his side Yvonne was staring before her with those wide-set, greenish eyes.

'Why did you do this?'

'You are being watched,' said Mannering simply. 'Didn't you see him?'

'*Watched*.' she repeated sharply. 'Why should I be?'

'I fancy your family will be watched for some time,' said the Baron. The thrill of the game, the exhilaration of knowing that every moment carried danger, every action had to be well-considered, was showing in his eyes. At moments like these he found it hard to believe that he had tried so often to push the Baron behind him, that only circumstances had forced him into action.

At Portland Place there was Fay Sharron, worried, anxious, mourning her dead lover and yet afraid of the truth she might learn about him; that truth was more likely to come through the Baron than any man. There was the dead Armstrong and the murdered girl, people for the Baron to avenge. There was the knowledge that Mendleson and Gillison were mixed up in the business, the murder as likely as the thefts. There was the strange case of Lord Sharron, another piece of the puzzle that could not yet be solved. And there were the Kallinovs to get back.

All part of the game, all making the Baron's interest deeper, bringing the light of battle to his eyes. And for the

98

moment the most important of the cyphers in the strange game was Yvonne, with her strange behaviour of the previous night, her unexpected talk of 'Bill', and those queerly intent green eyes now staring at him.

The Baron swung the car towards the Wandsworth Road, and glanced at the dashboard clock. They had been driving for two minutes. Within five Tring would have sent a call out for the car, it was not wise to stay in it long.

The girl said: 'You mean that? They are still watching us?'

Still, thought Mannering.

'Yes. How long have they been interested in your father?' She shrugged.

'How do I know? For some days, it would seem. Last night they expected to find the jewels.' She spoke with the slight breathlessness of one who was frightened and trying not to show it.

Mannering felt reassured: so it had been a raid against Gillison, there was no need to fear that his own visit had inspired Bristow's call.

'Did they?'

'No, of course not. Father isn't a fool.'

'I gathered that,' said the Baron drily. They had reached the road junction leading to West Hill, and he pulled into the kerb, after making sure that no policeman was in sight. She climbed out quickly, and hurried with him across the road. A bus had pulled up, going towards Tooting and Streatham.

They reached an almost deserted top deck, and selected a seat well away from anyone who might overhear them.

He said warningly: 'We've slipped the police, but they'll be watching for the car.'

She smiled for the first time; a quick, lively smile.

'You are a remarkable man, Baron.'

'Careful,' said the Baron, 'it's never wise to toss names about. I'm not so remarkable as experienced, Yvonne. Now—I've the money in my pocket. Not the notes that came from the safe, so you can use them safely. But before we reach that stage, I want you to talk. Why are you so anxious to get away?'

As the bus threaded its leviathan way through the traffic,

99

Yvonne told her story. It had the merits of simplicity, and Mannering believed her, searching in every sentence she uttered for something that might give him direct help in his quest.

It seemed she had little regard for her mother, and none for her father. Estelle Annette she dismissed with a grimace

'A *cocotte*, that is all. Father, of course, he knows it. He does not care. All he is interested in is money.'

The Baron could believe that.

Gillison had hidden the fact that he trafficked in stolen gems from his daughter and his wife, and Estelle knew nothing of it. Yvonne, more often at home, had not been so easily hoodwinked. She talked of three men who sometimes visited the house. Smith, tall, thin and hungry-looking. Mervin, fat and short, who lived in Mayfair and whom she dismissed with the same arrogance as she had dismissed Estelle. The third man had obviously impressed her.

'Rogerson is important. He works, I think, for my uncle, in his offices.'

The Baron's eyes narrowed, but he did not interrupt.

'You would always know him,' Yvonne said. 'He has a strange mouth, deformed I think.' Her voice altered, there was now an undercurrent of emotion in it. 'Then there was Bill.'

The Baron waited, his heart beating fast. The bus came to a standstill, people clattered up and down the stairs. The Baron swore beneath his breath, and with his mind on 'Bill', left the bus and hurried to the nearest tea-shop, in Streatham High Street. The tables were small, and well-spaced. He selected the most isolated and ordered tea and cakes.

He said easily, curbing his impatience: 'Now you can talk.'

Her words came in a spate. Bill Armstrong had come to Gillison for work. Among his other activities, Gillison controlled several small factories, all engaged in the manufacture of minor patents. Armstrong had been given a post at one of them, and:

'Sometimes Father sent for him. He came, of course. I— but what does it matter, he is dead. They killed him,

100

they——'

'Steady!' snapped Mannering. For the first time her control had broken, but she steadied herself immediately at his warning.

'I'm sorry, I will remember. He did not know, of course, how I felt. Why should he? Sometimes tea at the house, once he spent an evening there, and I—I was to find out many things about him. My father had asked—I had to do it. He was so difficult to talk to, so—so bitter. How did he know what I was thinking, how I wanted to help him? How could he know that I hated this woman he mentioned sometimes, this Fay? How could my father know it was torture to listen, to get him to talk?'

The Baron was sitting very still, for the girl's passionate sincerity stirred him.

'But he did talk?'

'Oh yes,' she said wearily. 'Of Lord Sharron, and his engagement. Then my father came in, talked of a way to make a fortune quickly. It was a week ago, perhaps a little more. The strong-room, said my father. Bill, he could get at it, learn the secrets——' Her eyes glowered, Mannering was prepared for something unexpected, and it came. 'The quarrel! I have never heard a man talk as Bill did to my father! *Tiens!* Father was furious, but he pretended that his suggestion was all a joke, that he wanted to make sure that he could trust Bill. I do not think that Bill believed it.'

Mannering was trying to fit this startling revelation in, seeing in it a possible vindication of Fay's belief in Armstrong.

Had Gillison eventually persuaded him?

'What happened, Yvonne?' he asked at last.

The fire had gone from her now.

'Bill, he left. Father, I knew, wished to dismiss him. I would not permit it. Bill was allowed to stay at his work, if he had not I would have made trouble. Then—the robbery. Bill died. My father says he knew nothing of it, says that he had seen Bill again, that Bill had agreed to help him. I shall never believe it.'

Mannering said: 'You're probably right, Yvonne. You didn't see Bill after that?'

101

'No, not even once. His photograph in the paper, that was how I learned. I thought'—the words came quietly—'that I would die. *Helas*, it is not so easy to die. But I could not sleep. For that reason I was up when you came last night. Always I carry a gun, for I know father sometimes is in danger. There are others who dislike him. I came, I saw you. I had heard, of course, of the Baron. At once I know why you come——'

Mannering broke in: 'How?'

'*Sacre Dieu*, to steal what he had stolen!'

The moment of alarm, the absurd feeling that she might have suspected he had come to regain his own jewels, died away.

'And immediately I think—I will help, for money. Father, he buys all I need, but gives me too little to spend. I had nothing to live in England for, I wanted to return to France. And so——' She lifted her hands, a pitiful little gesture, and a smile forced itself to her lips. 'You see?'

'Yes,' said Mannering slowly. 'You can get away, Yvonne, but if you are wise you will stay in this country for a while. The police will be watching you; they suspect your father and probably believe that you know what he does. Bank the money, and stay in England until it is all over. Will you do that?'

'I suppose it is wise.' Her voice was low, spiritless.

'It's essential,' said the Baron sharply. 'Don't go away, Yvonne, or they'll think you are frightened. Bank the money——'

'Will they know I have it?'

'They may find out, but I've arranged to cover you,' said Mannering, quietly. 'You've nothing to worry about. We'll talk of that later. First, Yvonne—does your father know the Baron?'

She stared.

'Know him? He has heard, of course, and talked about him, I have heard him say that he wishes he could work with him. But that is all.'

'You're sure?'

'That he does not know who you are? He has never said a thing to suggest he does. If he did know you he would have said so, why should he have kept quiet?'

102

That was logical, thought Mannering, but it did not answer the vital question: who had sent the note at Beverley? He had hoped to solve that problem, but it had to be shelved.

Meanwhile he had names to work on. Smith, Mervin and Rogerson.

He said slowly: 'Do you know where the jewels are?'

'They were at the house, or some of them. Smith had been trying to sell those which belonged to Mr. Mannering.' She was looking at him as the name came out, but there was no suggestion of recognition. 'Where they are now, I do not know. Father took them away.'

'When?'

'Soon after Smith had come back with them. Perhaps at eight o'clock. He received a telephone call, and then went out. That night I know he dined with my uncle, and they both came back to the house.'

'Is Mendleson concerned in this?' asked Mannering, more for formality's sake than anything else. He expected a quick 'yes', and he was startled when she said:

'With the thieving? No, of course not.'

The Baron drew a deep breath. If that was true it upset the whole fabric of his theories. He tried to make his voice sound casual as he asked:

'Are you sure?'

'*Tiens*, I cannot be so sure as that, Baron. But my father and uncle, they have work in common, but never has thieving been discussed between them. Uncle did not come that night because of the jewels, that I am certain. They have a scheme afoot, some company they are arranging. I know little about it. Lord Sharron and Lord Fauntley, they are interested.'

Mannering's mind reeled at the further shock.

'You're sure of that?'

'You are surprised?' Yvonne demanded, and he caught the shrewdness of her glance. 'Why should it interest you, it is not jewels.'

'No.' Mannering forced his voice to a tone of casual interest. 'But I am interested in your father, Yvonne, and others. This company—what do you know about it?'

'Why should you ask?'

'Isn't it enough,' asked the Baron, 'that I am giving you money for escape, Yvonne?' As he spoke he took an envelope from his pocket, and opened the flap. Inside she could see a thick wad of five- and ten-pound banknotes. Mannering put them in her hand.

'Of course,' she said, 'it is more than enough. I cannot thank you.' Tears sprang to her eyes.

'There's no need,' said Mannering, 'except to tell me all you can about this company.'

It was little enough.

Mendleson and Gillison were promoting it, and from Gillison's past efforts, and the suspicions that the Yard had of him, Mannering fancied that it was not what it appeared on the surface. Lord Sharron had been interested, as well as Fauntley, and with Mendleson would form the board—or so he inferred from her naïve statements. It was to do with some electrical manufacture, but on facts Yvonne was vague. She tried hard, clutching the envelope that spelled her freedom, and Mannering knew she was doing her best.

'And that is all I know,' she said at last.

She would need money in plenty if she was to go to France and live alone. She might be useful, but he did not propose to ask her to help him, it would be too dangerous; she had already shown her curiosity. Just one more question perhaps.

'You think your father arranged for Armstrong's death? What about the girl who was found murdered there?'

'Oh yes.' She spoke without enthusiasm, and he knew that she was brooding over Bill, and because of the depths of her feelings for the dead man, she would be likely to do incalculable things. He was more than ever convinced that he must not engage her active help. 'It was, I think, Mervin. He was to go and see her. The girl had been heard to talk to the young Sharron, she was looked on as dangerous, I don't know why. What are you staring at?'

Her voice sharpened and Mannering averted his eyes quickly.

'It doesn't matter. So Mervin was to go and see the girl, was he?'

Mannering barely listened to the answer. He was facing a startling fact.

104

Someone had overheard the murdered girl tell Reggie her story.

Someone in contact with Gillison had been at *Beverley Towers* when the girl had talked. All the guests had gone, there seemed no further doubt that Sharron or his wife or one of the servants was concerned, and he had been inclined from the first to rule out the servants.

If Yvonne's information was reliable, Armstrong had rejected the proposition.

And Mendleson, she was sure, was not directly connected with the robbery.

Was it Sharron?

CHAPTER FOURTEEN

BITS AND PIECES

Mannering did not return to the Park Lane flat, but with the help of a bottle of spirit in his pocket, cleaned off the greasepaint and other signs of the disguise at a cloakroom at Waterloo, and went to Brook Street. By that time Tring would have discovered the car, located the garage, and made his report, but it would not help the police. Yvonne had returned to Barnes. If the money was found she was to say that she had won it in betting, and Mannering had given her the name of a bookmaker who had the transactions on his ledgers, and would support her story if necessary. If she kept her head she would be safe enough.

As he suspected, Gillison was the instigator of the robbery. But the actual thief was still unknown, the jewels were as far away as ever, and Mannering believed that they would not remain in the country for long. To save them he must work fast.

He was dressing when a call came from Lorna with news he had half-expected. Fay was getting in an extremely overwrought state, and something must be done about it.

'I'll come over,' promised Mannering. 'About nine.'

Five minutes later the phone rang again. This time it was Leverson.

'Hello, Flick. News?'

'Of a kind,' said Leverson. 'I've nothing to help you directly, John, but I've discovered that Mendleson has a private secretary named Rogerson.'

The little pulse in the Baron's temple beat fast.

'And——?'

'Rogerson hasn't a good reputation. He was mixed up some time ago in a bucket-shop business, with a man named Mervin.'

'*What?*' That name again! 'Where can I find him?'

'He's in the phone book—Bewlay Mansions, I think, Mayfair. John, be warned by me, neither man is safe to play with.'

'I've guessed that,' Mannering said drily.

He put the receiver down thoughtfully. The thing which Yvonne had told him and which had startled him at the time, was growing more significant. Fauntley and Sharron, reputedly irreproachable, were apparently lined up with Mendleson and a company which had specialised in bucket-shop frauds.

Did Sharron's nervousness mean that he suspected the nature of the company that was to be promoted? If he was party to a coming fraud it would explain his nervousness, his loss of control. The more Mannering dwelt on Lord Sharron the more he doubted whether the man's recent activities could bear a close examination. For a moment he envied the police, who could have made an inquiry without the slightest trouble.

Fauntley, of course, could give him particulars of the company, but the only way to find the depths of Sharron's complicity was to raid his home.

And with the police concentrated about the *Towers* on the murder investigation, that was virtually impossible.

'Mervin and Rogerson first, I think,' murmured the Baron.

The dinner he had sent for from the restaurant was now brought in. Mannering went to his cocktail cabinet, and took the key out of his pocket. He frowned.

There were three or four minute scratches on the brass of the hole-piece.

He looked closer. The marks were obviously those of a pick-lock, used on the cabinet. It flashed through his mind that the police had paid him a visit, and there was a grim smile on his lips as he pulled at the door.

It jammed.

'Not Tring's work,' murmured the Baron, 'he's not so clumsy.'

A very faint, sweetish smell came from the cabinet. He left the door where it was, and stepped back, hearing a little hissing sound as he moved. It was gas of a kind; it had been put there so that on opening the cabinet he would breathe it in sharply: only death came to a man who breathed in prussic acid in any quantity.

He was alert for every possibility: *it was even possible that the man who had put it there was waiting in the flat.*

He had not been in the spare room, the man might be waiting there to see the results of this attempt—even to make it look like suicide: that had been tried on the Baron before. Keeping well away from the cabinet, he drew a deep breath, and wrenched the door open.

There was a sharp tinkle, the hissing grew louder and a cloud of gas billowed out. He dropped as it came, avoiding it. As he thudded to the floor, he moaned, simulating pain.

The hissing softened, died down.

Silence.

Then, softly, the sound of a door opening. He forced back a temptation to look round, as someone stepped from the bedroom.

Mannering heard the sound of a man's hushed breathing. A shadow fell across his head and shoulders, as the intruder passed the light. The shadow grew lower. Out of the corner of his eye Mannering could see the man's legs, saw him bending down, every movement soft and slow and dangerous.

Mannering felt a cold, intense anger. The would-be murderer was bending down, a hand was stretched out to touch Mannering's arm. Even now the movements were gradual, as though the other was half-fearful of a kick.

Mannering moved.

His hand gripped a hairy wrist with a fierce painful grip that made the other gasp. He twisted, sharply, intent on hurting. The man toppled forward, while Mannering sprang to his feet. The air was clear enough to breathe, although the faint smell of almonds still hung about the room. He saw the other's misshapen lips and knew that it was Rogerson.

Mannering's right fist shot out. He caught Rogerson beneath the chin. Rogerson grunted, and his eyes rolled. Mannering was filled with a fierce, savage anger, a desire to beat the man up, to make him suffer; but there was warning in his mind, too, an awareness of further danger.

He hit him again sending him reeling backwards. Mannering grabbed at his coat, in time to stop him from falling. He lowered him to the floor, then flung the window wide, welcoming the cold rush of air.

His singlet was clinging to him, as though he had been in an over-heated room. He loosened his collar and tie, and wiped his face with a handkerchief. Then, with a glance at the unconscious Rogerson, Mannering stepped to the cabinet.

The contraption was simplicity itself.

On a small square of wood stood a tin, and next to it a wine-glass was on its side. Water from it had spread about the wood and was dripping to the carpet. In the tin were several small pieces of what looked like wet soda. Mannering drew back hastily.

The fiendish cleverness of the trick appalled him.

The 'soda' was cyanide of potassium, of course, harmless when dry, but once the glass had been upset by the opening of the door prussic acid was generated by contact with water. A strong inhalation would have caused almost instantaneous death.

Despite the open windows the smell hung about the room.

Mannering realised that Rogerson must be one of the people who knew him as the Baron, might even be one of a dozen who knew that secret.

The danger had increased a hundredfold.

Mannering turned back to the tin. The quantity of the

gas generated had been too small to linger for long, only a sharp inward breath—natural in surprise—would have been sufficient to kill him. The nearness of the escape came back with redoubled force, the savage anger he had felt made the greater significance of Rogerson's presence fade.

He went into the bathroom, sponged his eyes with a weak boric acid mixture. There was no smell at all when at last he closed the window, dragged Rogerson from the floor and pushed him into an easy chair. He tied the man's ankles, to make a sudden movement impossible.

Leverson had warned him: the two murders—he was sure in his own mind of Armstrong's fate—should have been enough to have stopped him; but he had gone on and this was the result. He could not doubt that it was a direct answer from Gillison. Gillison knew him, knew of the danger he represented, and had sent Rogerson: there seemed no other explanation.

Could he force Rogerson to talk?

Talk of the police to a man who knew him for the Baron would be ineffective. Mannering was worried, and yet grimly determined to learn what Rogerson knew.

The man in the chair stirred.

Mannering lifted the telephone, and dialled Leverson's number. He did not appear to be watching Rogerson, but he saw the man's eyelids flicker, saw his hands grip the arms of the chair.

Leverson answered.

'Flick,' said Mannering slowly, 'I've an important job for you. It's one of the bunch we were talking about, and I want him well looked after ... yes, in London preferably ... he'll probably be obstinate, but he's got to talk.'

Leverson said: 'When will you bring him?'

'I can't be sure. Where's the best place?'

'*The Pitcher,*' said Leverson. 'I'll go there at once. Go into the private bar, and ask for me. Is he all right?'

'So far,' said the Baron, 'but whether he will be when I've finished with him I don't know.'

Putting down the receiver, Mannering stepped across the room, stood a yard from the other, and rasped:

'Who sent you?'

Rogerson shut his mouth in a tight line, both fear and

defiance clear in his eyes.

'There isn't the time nor the opportunity,' said the Baron in a hard, cold voice, 'to do what I want, Rogerson. But you're going to get rough treatment, and the longer you keep silent the rougher it will be.'

Fear was getting the upper hand.

'Don't be a fool!' The voice was thick, nasal. 'You daren't do anything, if you do I'll tell the police——'

Mannering's voice was whip-like.

'You'll tell the police what?'

'That—that you're the Baron! I tell you——'

He stopped, staring at Mannering's face which now showed a startled, incredulous expression, as though he could not believe his ears.

'I'm—*what*?'

'The Baron.'

Mannering laughed contemptuously.

'Someone's been pulling your leg. Who was it?'

Rogerson looked as startled as Mannering had done: he had believed Mannering to be the Baron but he did not know for sure. It was the first break Mannering had had that day. His spirits rose.

'You needn't trouble to call the police, I'll call them for you—when I've finished with you. But first, I want the story. When friends of mine get caught in a company racket run by two gentlemen like Gillison and Mendleson, I get worried. The police have tried to prove bucket-shop cases against them before, but they've failed. This time I'm keeping Fauntley and Sharron clear, and the way to do it is to prove it's a swindle, not talk about it. However——' He broke off, appearing not to watch the man, actually seeing every expression in the other's dark, close-set eyes. 'That won't interest you. Nothing is going to interest you for a long time.'

Rogerson's hard breathing filled the following pause.

He had shown enough to convince Mannering that he knew of the new company, and that it was a ramp, but at the menton of Fauntley and Sharron there had been no reaction. Mannering's own anxiety was to make Rogerson think he was interested only in the company angle, and he believed he was succeeding.

110

'Well,' said Mannering. 'Are you feeling more talkative?'

Rogerson said nothing. Mannering shrugged, and stepped to the window. He saw no one outside, but he believed Bristow would have a man watching back and front. With Rogerson in tow it would not be easy to dodge a trailer.

'No?' murmured the Baron. 'All right. You're coming with me, Rogerson. If you cause trouble, or if you make a break for safety and happen to get away, the police will be after you within ten minutes.' He stepped to the cabinet, picked up the whisky glass with his handkerchief, and brought it to Rogerson. 'Hold that.'

Rogerson reared up.

'No, no!'

'Don't be a damned fool, I'm not going to poison you. Hold it!'

Rogerson's fingers were trembling, but he obeyed. Mannering took the glass away, then pointed an unloaded revolver at Rogerson while he cut the cord at his ankles.

'Now open and close the cabinet.'

With a surly shuffle the man did so.

'Good. Your prints are on the glass and the wood: attempted murder carries a long sentence, Rogerson. Now get this into your head. We're going downstairs, and either walking to Piccadilly, or taking a taxi. If you try to dodge me, I'll shoot you, and then tell the police I was taking you to the Yard. Does it sink in?'

It seemed to do so. Mannering was relieved to find no watcher outside his flat.

Nor were they followed when a taxi took them to *The Pitcher*, a public house near Wine Street. The cab slowed down, and Mannering would have alighted but for the man standing on the kerb reading an evening paper.

It was Detective Inspector Moss: Drew and Edwards lounged near by.

CHAPTER FIFTEEN

COUNTER TRICK

Rogerson had made no protest, said not a word. Mannering felt alarm sear through him as he leaned forward, slid the partition back, and snapped to the driver:

'Make it Aldgate Station, please.'

Mannering was now fighting both sides; more than ever the need for relying almost entirely on himself impressed itself, as the need for making no single slip grew more urgent.

He did not believe it was a coincidence that the police were in force at *The Pitcher*. Word had got through, and the men had been taken from Brook Street merely to lull him into a state of false security. It was touch and go all the time, with Bristow, and every move could spell disaster.

What should he do now?

Rogerson stirred, glancing from the window. Mannering felt the tension in the other, sensed what was in his mind.

Mannering slid open the partition again.

The cabby turned his head, showing a bored face resigned to the eccentricities of his fares.

'Yessir?'

Where, where, where? The question flooded Mannering's mind. Three direct problems faced him. To avoid *The Pitcher* and therefore the police; to find Leverson and get Rogerson to a place of safety; and to prevent the man from knowing that his captor was afraid of the police—if, indeed, it was not already too late for that.

He took a chance, keeping his voice low.

'Nineteen Wine Street, do you know it?'

The cabby nodded, turned a corner sharply, and drew up outside Leverson's house.

Mannering glanced about him, making sure that there was no one in sight. The police might be watching, but they had probably kept away from Leverson's place as well as his.

He paid the cabby, and pushed Rogerson forward. As he

did so, the front door of the house opened, and he was relieved to recognise the trim figure of Janet, Leverson's maid. Janet had served the fence for years: Leverson had saved her father from prison, for that Janet was prepared to serve him to the end of time. She was no more than twenty-five, pert, neat, friendly, and with all the nimble-wittedness of the native East Ender.

'Good evening, Mr. Mannering.'

'Hallo, Janet. Mr. Leverson's expecting me'

'He's——'

'Out, I know, but I'll wait.'

She nodded and drew aside. Rogerson and the Baron went into the drawing-room where Mannering had talked with Leverson on his return to London. Only the firelight illuminated it at first, lending the room a homely, mellow atmosphere of rest and ease.

Janet switched on the light and the illusion vanished. Rogerson's dark face registered danger; he was kept in check only because of the fingerprints on the glass and cabinet. Janet eyed him inquiringly.

'He was to meet me at *The Pitcher*,' Mannering said, 'but I preferred to come straight here.'

'I'll send a message,' promised Janet.

Mannering had reason to know how reliable she was in emergency, and he felt happier as he followed her into the hall, and whispered:

'Tell him *The Pitcher*'s surrounded.'

Her eyes widened, but she nodded comprehendingly.

Rogerson was on his feet, and a torrent of words greeted Mannering as he re-entered the room.

'You can't do it, I tell you you can't do it, they'll fix you, I'll see to that, they'll fix you!'

Mannering said: 'We'll know better what to do with you in a few days, Rogerson. Tonight's little game at Brook Street will stop me from worrying overmuch.' He spoke coldly, dispassionately, praying that his bluff would succeed. 'I've been watching you, as Mendleson's right-hand man, and I've wanted this talk. The prussic acid gives it more point, that's all. If you talk, and if it's the truth, I might let you go. Who pitched the fairy story that I was the Baron?'

113

Rogerson gulped.

'I'm not talking!'

They waited in silence until Leverson walked into the room.

'There's our man,' Mannering said, 'if you can look after him for a bit, we'll fix details later.'

'Yes, I'll do it,' Leverson promised.

Mannering was startled. Flick's voice had altered; it held a sharpness that was not far from viciousness as he stared at Rogerson.

'I could doubtless persuade him to talk now,' said Leverson, in that dead cold voice, 'if you can stay.'

'I'm in a rush, Flick.'

'A pity.' Leverson sounded regretful as they turned away. At the door he muttered: 'Moss is still at *The Pitcher*, but you weren't recognised.'

'You saw me?'

'I saw the cab. I'll phone you later, at the call-box.'

'So they've tapped the wire?'

'Yes.' Leverson turned back to Rogerson, while Mannering went out.

He had little cause to feel elated. Bristow was using his heavy artillery, watching everywhere and taking no chances. Gillison had proved his ruthlessness. To win any chance at all, the Baron had to work fast and strike where it was least expected.

Leverson had scared him, and would have scared most men with that slow, cold, cruel voice. A surprising man, Flick Leverson, used to dealing with all kinds of emergency, yet mellow and suave and never ruffled.

At nine o'clock to the minute Mannering was ringing the bell at Portland Place.

As Parker opened the door Mannering heard Fauntley's voice, querulous and sharp.

'But I tell you they *must* be found. My dear Sharron——'

'Miss Lorna is upstairs, sir,' said Parker, 'if you'd care to go straight up.'

'Tell her I'll be up soon,' said Mannering. 'Announce me downstairs now, will you?'

'Very good, sir.'

Fauntley, breaking off his conversation with Sharron, gave a nod and a half-smile.

'Hallo, John.'

Mannering gave an answering greeting, then turned to Sharron.

'Hallo, Sharron, I've been going to see Reggie all day, but haven't managed it. Have you been?'

The peer was looking very uneasy, Mannering also thought that he looked ill.

'Not yet,' he said. 'I'm going on from here. Good of you to look after him, Mannering.'

'I've been saying, the police must find the stones,' Fauntley broke in, impatient to get at the subject closest to his heart. 'Five days, and not a sign. They'll be out of the country if we're not careful.'

'No one's more sorry about it than I am, Fauntley,' said Sharron sharply. 'But talking like this leads us nowhere. Obviously the work was done by expert jewel-thieves, we must give the police time. After all, we were insured.'

'*Insured?* And will money give me back the Leopolds? The only emeralds authoritatively connected with the Russian Crown in this country!'

'For God's sake shut up!' roared Sharron.

He was on his feet, glaring at the startled Fauntley. Mannering had never seen a man nearer breaking point, and he wondered what was causing it. Not worry about the jewels, he was sure of that. It was the moment he had been waiting for, the chance to catch Sharron off his guard.

'There are other things,' he said soothingly. 'For instance, have you heard rumours about Mendleson?'

Sharron flinched, his whole bearing betraying the shock of the words. In that moment the Baron was convinced of Sharron's complicity in one game or the other.

'What about him?' gasped Fauntley.

Mannering said easily: 'Rumours, and strong ones, that he's up to some chicanery with a new company. He——'

'*What?*' yelled Fauntley. 'You mean to say *that's* unsound?'

Sharron had dropped back into his chair, was trying hard to regain his lost composure as Mannering said:

'There's reason to believe it, anyhow. I don't know any-

115

thing about the company, but I did hear that Sharron was on the board.' He looked inquisitively at Sharron, but it was Fauntley who answered.

'He wás,' snapped Fauntley, 'and so was I. Am, I mean —look here, John, if it's true I mu t see him. But I can't believe—damme, it's a quarter of a million pound issue, we've even rented factories, placed orders for machinery!'

'The rumours *are* about,' said Mannering.

'It's madness! I tell you I've every confidence in the company—it's to manufacture electrical parts essential for aeroplanes and cars, it has already secured Government orders. I must see Mendleson at once.'

Orders obtained through Fauntley, thought Mannering, and he watched Sharron, who had gone very white but was making a strong effort to regain his composure.

'Nonsense, Fauntley, you can't talk to him about rumours.'

'*Can't* I! I've already advanced twenty thousand! I— John, this can't be true! It must be some absurd mistake!'

Mannering shrugged.

'Possibly. I'll find what I can by tomorrow, and let you know. Is Lorna in?'

'Yes, upstairs.'

As Mannering left the room he heard Fauntley's voice raised again in indignation. He hurried up the stairs and found Lorna and Fay together.

'I can't stay for more than a minute,' he told them, 'but I've news of a sort.'

Fay was on her feet in an instant, looking at him with a queer, intense expression.

'About Bill?'

'I have it on good authority,' said Mannering, 'that he was asked to help in the robbery, and turned the offer down. Abruptly, I gather. If he did anything he shouldn't, it was in keeping the suggestion from the police.'

'So he refused,' Fay said in a low voice, 'and they killed him to prevent him from talking. Who are they?'

He wondered what would happen if eventually it was proved that her father had been in the conspiracy, but he pushed the thought aside.

'I'm not sure, Fay, I can't work miracles. Meanwhile you

116

won't leave here, please. You might telephone Reggie, he helped me to get at the facts. You won't get him, of course, but there's a nurse on duty all the time. Done?'

Before she could speak again he was gone.

Striding towards Piccadilly, Sharron's car passed him. Immediately he sprinted to a coasting taxi and wrenched the door open.

'Keep that car in sight,' he snapped.

Five minutes later, the Rolls pulled up outside Mendleson's house in South Audley Street.

Yvonne had assured Mannering that Mendleson knew nothing of the robbery. Yet surely, Mannering thought, his presence at Castelnau had been too soon after the affair to be fortuitous?

Was Mendleson holding the diamonds?

Did he know that Rogerson had been to visit Mannering, and on what errand?

Was it too risky to visit Mendleson by night?

The Baron very much disliked the idea. Such a house was usually backed by a courtyard, and frequently a labyrinth of passages. Yet it seemed increasingly certain that Mendleson was the key to the whole business. Mannering stopped the cab, but hesitated; he had no tools with him. The front door lock of the house was unlikely to be difficult. Should he take the risk of getting in and trying to overhear the conversation?

He knew that such an undertaking was madness, but it was a fact that he had an opportunity unlikely to come again. The two men perhaps most vitally concerned were at that moment in earnest discussion.

To break in was a risk no greater than he had taken a dozen times in the past. He had a scarf in his pocket, which he could easily use for a mask.

The cabby shifted irritably.

'All right,' said Mannering sharply, and his heart was pounding as he climbed out and walked back along the road. An iron gate, four steps and the front door. People were passing to and fro, cars went by with their lights glowing. The street lamps spread a brilliance, making everything clear.

117

The very audacity of it would get him over the first hurdle.

Now that his mind was made up he pushed all thought of the risk aside, drugging his reason with the excuse that speed was all important. When he reached the front door he had his penknife in his hand.

The lock was old-fashioned and simple: he took less than ten seconds to push it back and open the door.

A dim light shone from the hall. Mannering listened, but heard no sound other than the murmur of voices muffled by a closed door. He slipped the scarf over his face so that only his eyes showed.

He was keyed up to a high stretch now, but his chief thought was of the conversation coming from a room on the left of the hall. It was loud enough for him to catch an occasional word.

He reached the door.

Tensely he tried the handle. The door opened.

Sharron was saying excitedly: 'But I tell you it's true! Mannering's heard the rumour, you've got to get me out of it!'

'Mannering hasn't heard the rumour,' said Mendleson clearly, 'because there isn't one. He's seen you are jittery, and it appears that he's interested in me, though not, perhaps, as much as I am interested in him.'

'But why should he be? Answer me that!'

Mendleson swore.

'That blasted robbery! If I knew who'd been to the *Towers* I'd break their necks! A lot of publicity was the last thing I wanted. Oh, I saw on Tuesday that Mannering believed Armstrong had been murdered, and he's played some fool detective games in the past. The man's a lot too swollen-headed, it'll be a pleasure to clip his wings.'

'And how will you do that, pray?'

'Slander,' snapped Mendleson, tersely.

There was silence from the room now, as though the others were giving Mannering breathing space as well as themselves. And he needed it! If Mendleson was not acting, he knew nothing of the robbery. That confirmed Yvonne's opinion. It meant that Sharron knew nothing, it meant that Mendleson had no idea of Rogerson's attempt

118

to kill him, although Rogerson was his private secretary.

And if he was prepared to take action for slander it suggested that the company could bear any investigation.

Mannering's carefully built-up theories were blown away. He would have to cast round for another explanation. Already possible suspects were running through his mind. Gillison, of course, at the head. Mervin—he had not seen the man yet—Reggie Sharron, even Theo Crane.

He would——

Footsteps came, soft and nearby.

The Baron stiffened, aware of his own danger. At the top of the stairs he saw the legs and feet of a man, coming quickly down.

CHAPTER SIXTEEN

MR. LANCELOT MERVIN

Between safety and discovery there was a fraction of a second, and Mannering was not sure whether it was enough. He moved backwards with three short, swift steps, and stood against the panelling that ran beneath the staircase. If the man had glanced down at that moment the alarm would have been raised; as it was the soft footsteps continued, very close to Mannering's head, and the Baron's hands were clenched to meet the trouble if it came.

Had he been seen?

The man hesitated at the foot of the steps, and then stepped forward, towards the front door. The Baron glanced beyind him, but there was nowhere he could hide. A door, leading to a cupboard wardrobe under the stairs was ten feet along the passage, too far away for him to reach in safety.

The front door opened, and the chill air came in, fluttering the scarf about Mannering's face. The servant stood for

119

a moment on the threshold, and Mannering could hear him sniffing the night air. And at the same time a chair scraped from the room where Sharron and Mendleson had been talking.

Mannering moved.

He reached the door. The man heard him, and turned about. He saw the tall man in evening dress, and the mask: and then the tall man's fist shot out, and hit him scientifically on the solar plexus. Before he could fall, the baron caught him, reversed positions, lowered him gently, and stepped across the threshold.

He hurried down the steps, turning right towards a side turning. A cruising taxi slowed down.

'London Pavilion,' said the Baron.

The impulse to risk such a visit had been justified. He was doubly glad now that he had taken the chance.

How far had he committed himself?

Could Mendleson take an action for slander on the strength of that brief conversation?

Was Mendleson quite guiltless of conspiracy in both the robbery and the company?

They were questions it was impossible to answer immediately. He was inclining more and more to the theory that Sharron was a party to the theft, without Mendleson's knowledge, but the issues were getting hopelessly confused, and he was as far away from the jewels as when he had started.

At a telephone booth he looked up Mervin. An uncommon name, he found, and there was only one in residence at Bewlay Mansions, Mayfair; his Christian name was Lancelot.

Mervin looked at the ringing telephone with reproachful eyes.

The brilliantly painted room held a nightmarish quality which was increased by Mervin, as he sat back on an Oriental divan, sandals on his plump feet, a green dressing-gown embroidered with red dragons about his tubby form. In his fingers, very fat and white, was the end of an opium dipper.

Regretfully, reproachfully, Mervin rested the dipper in

the glass jar of opium, and slid from the divan. Softly he lifted the receiver of the telephone.

'This is Lancelot Mervin.'

'Have you seen Rogerson?' Gillison's voice came sharply.

Mervin's eyes narrowed, as though pained by the other's abruptness.

'No, no, not since six o'clock, my friend.'

'Has he reported?'

'Not, I'm afraid, to me.'

'We've got to find him,' snapped Gillison. 'He should have been back by now. Where did he go, do you know?'

'Unfortunately he did not confide in me. Such a pity, but a self-willed gentleman, as you know. Did he not give you any information?'

'He said he knew where to find the Baron,' Gillison grunted.

'Yes, of course. He even admitted that to me. But nothing more. I am convinced, my friend, that he plans to blackmail the Baron, and is very anxious that no one should share the ample proceeds.'

'You're way out,' said Gillison grimly. 'He wasn't going to work him. I'd told him what to do.'

There was a moment's silence, and then Mervin's lips twitched.

'I see, my friend, I see. Taking no chances, eh? Or possibly changing them for others.'

'Don't blether,' said Gillison. 'Rogerson was due at ten o'clock. If the damned fool had told me the name I could make inquiries.'

'So unfortunate,' crooned Mervin, 'that Rogerson works so much on his own. So inconsiderate. But still he has a remarkable way of coming successfully through these various crises. I expect he will appear again. Er—my dear Gillison, I am a little worried, just a little worried. My safe is a teeny bit overloaded at the moment. You will try to relieve the pressure in the near future, I trust.'

'It's all right there for the time being.'

'Yes. But think of the Baron, my friend, if he took it into his head to pay me a visit, how disastrous it would be.'

'He can't know you,' snapped Gillison.

'But can you be sure?' Mervin sighed. 'Is there anything else?'

'If Rogerson phones you, ring me at once.'

Mervin replaced the instrument slowly, and looked at the divan, with its rich silks and draperies. His eyes, brown, soulful, carrying the indefinite signs of a drug-addict, widened. Regretfully he put out the lamp, placing it, with the pipe, in a cabinet of ebony, exquisitely carved.

Every movement was slow, yet despite his uncouth figure he had a feline grace; uncanny, to some people frightening. Wrapping the dressing-gown more tightly about him, he opened a door and stepped through into what appeared to be a music-room. In one corner stood a Bechstein grand, near it a set of Chinese reed pipes. Lining one wall was a rack used for keeping music. Of the three easy-chairs only one was occupied, and that by a woman. She was plump and shapeless, and sleeping heavily.

Mervin touched her shoulder. Her eyes flicked open.

'What is it, dear, what is it?'

'I would like you to sing, Clara,' said Mervin gently.

She rubbed her eyes, looked about her, as though only half-awake, then moved to the piano. The first strains of Schubert's *Der Jangling und Der Tong* drifted slowly and exquisitely into the room.

At one o'clock that morning the Baron entered Bewlay Mansions.

In the night-porter's cubby-hole a man was dozing in front of a gas fire, and the Baron's rubber-soled shoes made no sound on the stone floor. Even if the porter had looked up he would have seen only a portly, middle-aged gentleman entering the Mansions so openly that no suspicions would have been aroused.

The Baron located Flat 17, which was on the second floor.

It could be approached by the stairs and by an automatic lift, and he chose the stairs. The wide passage which led to three other flats, was carpeted. No sound was coming from the right or left, and no gleams of light showed. He approached Number 17 quickly, and examined the lock.

It was a Yale, and therefore could not be picked by a

skeleton key. If he attempted other means the noise might disturb a dozen people; in any case it would take him twenty minutes, while if anyone passed while he was inside the flat the damage to the lock would be noticed immediately.

Quickly he walked to the end of the passage, making a mental drawing of the layout of the floor. A door leading to the fire-escape opened without trouble. Mannering slipped outside. A faint glow, coming through thick curtains, showed at one window.

He identified the lighted window quickly: it was one opening from Mervin's flat. Its neighbour was in darkness, and from it led another fire-escape.

The Baron hurried down to the courtyard, and climbed the second flight of iron stairs. As he reached the landing outside the flat he stood and looked down. The street lamps spread only a faint light, and he could no longer see them, which meant that he could not be seen from the streets. There were no lights at the windows opposite.

He slipped the scarf mask over his face.

The window he had chosen to be his means of entry was in small panes, about nine inches high by five across, and the framework was of iron. The catch was on the left-hand side.

From his tool-kit he took a sheet of brown paper, and damped a side already gummed with a sponge taken from a wash-leather bag. He stuck the paper over the pane nearest the catch, left it for a few seconds, and took a rubber-handled screwdriver from his pocket.

Although he had believed there were no sounds he was faintly aware of a woman's voice singing.

Sharply, he struck the paper with the screwdriver handle.

There was a dull *crack,* noise enough to make him turn and scan the courtyard below, but after thirty seconds no sound of alarm disturbed him. He turned back to the window, and pulled the paper away, and the noise was hardly audible. When the paper was in his hand, pieces of glass were sticking to it.

He cleared the leaded frame, then slid his hand inside the broken window.

There was no noise as he lowered the catch, no sign of a

123

wire alarm. He used his torch, making sure there was no alarm inserted against the outside frame. Satisfied, he pushed the window open. A heavy curtain hung inside, and he pushed it back before climbing through.

From the far end of the room came a glimmer of light, barely discernible, while the singing grew louder. He moved towards the door, where he expected to find the light switch. He succeeded, and a soft light flooded the room.

Mannering stood and stared.

A faint smell hung about the room, almost like incense, but apart from the crumpled cushions of the divan and the red telephone in one corner, there was no sign of occupation. He opened a small door and found that it led through a kitchen to the front door of the flat. It was locked and bolted, and wired for alarm. He snapped the wire with his cutters, drew the bolts, and unlatched the door before turning back to the room he had left.

His eyes ran over the ebony cabinet as he registered the fact that opium had been recently smoked.

All the time the faint strains of music and a voice raised in song came to his ears. To reach the bedroom where the safe was likely to be, he had to pass through the next room. Should he wait, hoping that Mervin and the woman would go to bed? Or should he put a scare into them?

Mannering's eyes narrowed, and very softly he touched the handle of the door. When it was open a fraction of an inch singing came more clearly.

He had heard the voice before.

He knew that, but could not recall where. No matter. He slipped his right hand into his pocket and drew out a gun. It was unloaded—the Baron knew better than to risk being caught with a loaded firearm in his possession—but it looked dangerous. Handy, too, was the gas-pistol.

He opened the door wider, and slipped through.

The man was sitting sideways to the door, the woman was looking at him.

The Baron stood very still, trying to believe his eyes.

It was Mendleson's wife; he knew now where he had heard the voice before, and in his mind's eye there was a picture of that night at *Beverley Towers*.

Did *this* explain the mystery?

124

He had ignored the women as suspects, but Clara Mendleson and Mervin here together, at nearly two o'clock, suggested a long association.

At a slight sound, the woman swung round, a scream at her lips, but it stopped as the Baron moved his gun. Mervin only turned his head. Mannering saw those sleepy, unnatural eyes, knew that the man was drugged. He said sharply:

'Start playing again.'

A moment's hesitation, and then the man obeyed. The Baron was thinking fast, wondering whether to make them unconscious before searching the bedroom, or to make Mervin open the safe. It was uncanny to feel those sad eyes fixed on his.

Before he spoke again, Mervin opened his lips.

'And what, my friend, have you done with Rogerson?'

The Baron's grip on his gun tightened.

'I've come to get——'

'The jewels, of course, the lovely jewels!'

But with the silky words there came to the Baron an uneasy feeling of distrust; the room held a menace he could not explain, but it filled him with an unreasoning fear. And all the time Mervin's strange eyes were fixed on his, and the woman sat there shaking.

CHAPTER SEVENTEEN

NO ESCAPE?

The effect of the unspoken menace remained for what seemed an unconscionable time. The Baron believed he understood it when Mervin began to strum a nonsense melody that increased the atmosphere of unreality. The man was mad.

'You seem disturbed, my friend,' said Mervin softly.

'You need not be. The jewels are here, or those with which I was trusted.'

'Where is the safe?'

'A problem, my friend, but won't you sit and listen to——'

Mad? He was as sane as Mannering, but he was bluffing; just for a moment his eyes had glinted with a natural cunning. His voice had grown sharper, too. Mannering shivered uncontrollably.

'Stand up, Mervin, with your back to me.'

'But, my friend——'

'Stand up!' The gun moved to give force to the words, and Mervin lifted his hands from the keys, and rose slowly.

'Walk towards me, backwards,' ordered the Baron.

His left hand went into his pocket for the gas-pistol, but he did not draw it out until Mervin was within a yard of him. He expected a trick from the man, but none was tried.

'Stop,' said Mannering.

A scream, stifled at birth, came from the woman's lips as he pulled out the gas-pistol, and at the same moment swung Mervin round. Automatically the man drew an inward breath, and he took the full force of the ether gas. He staggered, his hands moved, and then he slumped into a nearby chair. His breathing grew heavier. Mannering watched him struggling against the inevitable unconsciousness.

Mannering turned to the woman.

'Come here,' he said. 'It won't hurt, you'll be asleep for a few minutes, that's all.'

'No, no, I daren't!'

He stepped towards her swiftly, and although she threw up her hands to try to save herself, the gas worked quickly. As he lowered her to a chair he saw that her lips had acquired a bluish tinge. He dared not use chloroform, for even under the ether her pulse was beating too fast, and for her to die under the anaesthetic would amount to murder. He did not think she presented much danger, but he tied her ankles together, not too tightly, and her wrists.

He dosed Mervin with chloroform.

Now that they were both unconscious and he had the flat to himself, the peculiar feeling of unreality had disappeared. But its influence remained.

126

Did Mervin know or suspect the identity of the Baron?

He stepped into the bedroom. It was decorated in futuristic splashes of vari-coloured paint, and he saw with relief that it was surprisingly empty of clutter.

It was impossible to say from a glance at the walls that there was no wall-safe. One might be hidden behind the paintwork, merging with it so as to be discerned only with difficulty. Mervin had admitted the jewels were here.

Had he lied?

The Baron half-wished that he had forced the man to reveal his safe, but he was glad that Mervin was unconscious. Those queer eyes worried him, even in retrospect. If it were possible to find an atmosphere of evil, Mannering believed that it was here: the place was bad.

He worked systematically at the walls, running the palm of his gloved hands over every square inch, without result. Puzzled, he searched the drawers of two small chests. Neither of them yielded what he wanted; both were movable, not fixed to the wall as he had at first suspected. Nor was there any room for a false drawer or a sliding panel. More puzzled than before, he went back into the music room, but a search there revealed nothing that might help him find the safe.

He tried the floors, but the rubber was in one piece, joined to the rubber of the walls. Mervin had made the flat virtually soundproof; even the doors were lined with rubber, which overlapped on all sides, excluding both draught and sound.

The search grew more fantastic with the passing minutes.

The silence, too, was unnatural. He glanced at his watch and saw that it was half-past two. An hour's search, without result.

He examined the piano, but found no evidence of a secret hiding place.

Three o'clock came.

Mannering was beginning to fall under the spell of the apartment, and the apparently non-existent safe added to his disquiet. He stripped the beds, but the framework was of tubular steel. The mattresses yielded nothing.

There was nothing in the room he had not examined.

At half-past three, working all the time in an atmosphere

127

of unreality that was rapidly getting on his nerves, he looked again at his watch, then glanced up sharply at the clock set in the wall.

It was set against a patch of vermilion red and seemed genuine enough. But he worked at it swiftly, prising the glass open.

With a small screwdriver, he took out the screws holding the clock to the wooden base behind it. The uncertainty, the menace of the flat was back in his mind. He was hardly breathing, for the suppressed excitement and the possibility that he had found what he wanted merged together in a high tension.

And then the tension broke, with a sharp hiss.

Automatically he ducked, but not before he had seen the white vapour spitting out, nor before the gas had bitten at his eyes. He clenched his teeth to stop from crying out with the sharp pain, as he reeled backwards.

He hit against a bed and collapsed on it, holding his head in his hands. He recognised the symptoms of tear-gas, thanking heaven that the mask had protected him from a stronger dose.

He had no idea how long he was sitting there, but gradually his sight came mistily back to him. Rising unsteadily he groped his way to the bathroom. Among the jars and lotions he at last found what he wanted, a bottle of boric acid crystals. He made a solution in lukewarm water, and the relief to his eyes was immediate.

Five minutes later he was nearly normal.

When he reached the music-room again, Mervin was conscious. His lips curved in a gentle smile.

'Not too unpleasant I trust, my friend?'

'Experience is nearly always useful,' said Mannering drily, 'I won't be unprotected another time.' he bent down, tested the bonds, and went back into the bedroom.

The tear-gas had expended itself, and Mannering found the door of the safe behind the lock easy to open. It was larger than he had expected, and it contained both jewel-cases and papers. Mannering cleaned it out, replaced a wad of notes, and then examined the cases.

His hands were trembling a little, but he knew after a quick inspection that he had found most of what he wanted.

Fauntley's Leopolds winked up, their lambent green like winking eyes. The Delling stones, a diamond string, were there: so were Crane's rubies, and Mendleson's mixed collection, all fine gems. A fortune for the taking!

He checked them over, and when he had finished he frowned. The only stones missing except the Kransits, which Leverson had held temporarily, were his own Glorias.

'Which has its amusing side,' said the Baron aloud.

'And so has this,' said Mervin from the door.

The Baron swung round. Mervin, legs and arms free, was standing in the doorway. In his hand was an automatic.

The Baron did not stir. Mervin's eyes were hard, now, showing no softness.

'Take off your mask.'

Mannering obeyed. There was no object in refusing, and no one would recognise him as Mannering. Mervin nodded.

'A surprise, my friend? You perceive the impossible?'

'The unlikely,' Mannering said with an effort.

'Ah. So you believe that all things have a material explanation, Baron? I could discuss the matter at some length, some of my experiences in the Darker World would, I am sure, interest you. But at the moment I had best concern myself with facts. You are in an extremely difficult position—but of course you realise that.'

Mannering said more easily: 'I've been in worse.'

Mervin shook his head.

'You know, I find that difficult to believe. Where is Rogerson?'

'Who?'

Mervin's eyes narrowed.

'Such ignorance seems a trifle puerile, Baron. Rogerson, Mr. Mendleson's so admirable secretary. Surely you know he has been to visit you?'

'I do not,' said the Baron sharply.

The immediate shock was over. He was facing a gun, which was ominous enough, but something he could deal with in emergency. Mervin's escape from the cords must be explained later. Meanwhile it was necessary to deny seeing Rogerson. He must do nothing to confirm the belief that Mannering was the Baron.

129

'I—see,' drawled Mervin. 'Is it possible that our friend has made a mistake? When did you leave your flat?'

'I haven't got one.'

'No? Rogerson said distinctly that he was to visit your flat, but he omitted to say where, and he omitted to mention your name. It sounds——'

'Rogerson can't know me,' snapped the Baron.

'No? And why?'

'No one does.'

'I see.' Mervin nodded. 'I soon will, my friend, very soon I'm afraid. However, it gives me some pleasure to believe that Rogerson and—ah—others have made a mistake, they are so hot-headed, so confident of their invulnerability. Not unlike yourself, perhaps. You have a long if dishonourable career behind you, and it will be a pity to spoil it. However——'

'You can hardly go to the police,' said Mannering, 'with most of the stuff from Beverley here.'

'Ah, but it won't be here when the police come, my friend. Tell me——' He dismissed the subject drily. 'How did you know that I might have the jewels?'

'I'd seen you going to Gillison's place.'

'And Rogerson?'

'I don't remember him.'

'A rather fearsome-looking creature with a twisted lip.'

'Oh, him!' said the Baron with a convincing expression of surprise. 'Lives in a house in South Audley Street. I don't like City jobs'.

'Well, well,' murmured Mervin. 'So there are some tasks too difficult even for the venturesome Baron?'

'Supposing you cut the cackle,' snapped Mannering.

'A little worried?' murmured Mervin. 'Understandable, I suppose. If you will be good enough to hand me those cases, we will move on to the next development quickly.'

Mannering hesitated.

'At once,' snapped Mervin, and the gun lifted.

It was the one moment when the Baron had a chance, and he knew that no matter how slender, he had to take it. He shrugged his shoulders, and held the cases towards Mervin who stretched his free hand for them. Their fingers were touching when Mannering jerked his hand up, and the

130

cases went into Mervin's face. The man fired, but Mannering had dodged to one side. Before he could snatch the gun away Mervin had fired twice again, the bullets thudding into the rubber flooring.

Mannering hit him.

Mervin staggered, his head jolting back, the gun and cases falling to the floor. Mannering scooped them up, stuffing them into his pockets, then rushed into the next room shutting the door behind him. The key was in the lock, and he turned it. He felt reasonably sure there would be no immediate alarm, for the flat was virtually sound-proof; the broken window might let the echoes of the bullet shots get outside, however, and he had no time to lose.

Clara Mendleson had not moved, but Mervin's cords were on the floor, burned through. On the small table next to the piano was a petrol lighter. The flame was burning, ample evidence of how the man had freed himself.

Mannering swung towards the hall.

As he went he saw that the front door was ajar, and before he reached it he heard footsteps pounding up the staircase, along the passage. Voices were raised, too, and Mannering realised his mistake. By leaving the front door on the latch he had destroyed the muffling effect of the rubber flanges. Mervin had not known that, or he would not have dared to shoot. It meant a police inquiry, and Mervin would have a lot to explain, but there was barely time for the Baron's own getaway, which was his chief concern.

He made for the opened window, climbing through to the fire-escape.

He was in the courtyard before he saw a man's head and shoulders against the light which had leapt into the window of Mervin's flat. Moving fast he reached the doorway at the far end of the yard. He had examined the plan of the mansions and precincts, and knew that the alleyway led to some mews at the back of South Audley Street. The door was neither locked nor bolted. He went through, hearing the sharp impact of leather heels on the steel of the fire-escape.

At the Mews he turned towards South Audley Street, dropping to a brisk walk.

The sounds of pursuit had died away.

Breathing hard, and perspiring freely, he cut across the

131

street to a narrow turning that would take him towards Park Lane. Five minutes of walking brought him out near Fuller Mansions.

Less than half an hour after leaving Mervin, he was sitting in the flat of Mr. Moore, fingering the Kransit diamonds, which he had arranged with Leverson would be waiting for him. Quickly he addressed three envelopes, slipping a case into each, and went out to post them.

Back in the flat, he was asleep inside ten minutes.

Superintendent Lynch of Scotland Yard, large, placid and good-natured, blinked at Bristow.

'Well, Bill, what's new?'

Bristow lit a cigarette, and eyed the smoke reflectively.

'If the man's to be trusted, the Baron visited him last night.'

'Any reason why you shouldn't believe him?'

'Dozens. The flat gave me the horrors, and the certainty that Mervin is not a nice man to know. Opium, among other things. I've got full particulars, after an hour's questioning. He's independent—pretty well-off in fact—and an amateur musician. He has a fancy safe, in the form of a clock operated by mechanism, and tear-gas comes out when it is opened without a key.'

Lynch leaned forward intently.

'Did it come out last night?'

'Yes. He says the Baron took it in his eyes. It played old Harry with the disguise, but I can't get a worthwhile description. There *had* been a raid, but Mervin doesn't seem clear on what's missing. He's much too vague.' Bristow spoke irritably. 'He might have dreamed the blue mask, but—well, there was a woman there. A queer business. She'd been dosed with ether gas, and he'd been chloroformed.'

'It sounds like Mannering,' said Lynch.

'Could be, but I'd be happier if I didn't think Mervin was a first-class liar. I think he's hiding something. But there is one thing that makes me feel Mannering might have been there.'

'Well?'

'The woman was Mendleson's wife.'

Lynch sat up sharply.

'So there's a Beverley connection.'

'I don't know what to make of it,' Bristow admitted irritably. 'Apparently the Mendlesons don't live together, but they keep up appearances when they go visiting. She and Mervin seem to have been intimate for some time. She's got a voice, y'know, and he's something of a pianist.'

Lynch sniffed.

'If the Baron went there, it's almost certainly because he thinks Mervin was connected with the Beverley job. Mannering's after those jewels. I wish——' He hesitated.

'All right, Bill, don't be shy.'

Bristow glanced up in annoyance.

'I was going to say that I wish I could trust the Baron to send those jewels where they belong. If he did that I'd be inclined to let him have a run, up to a point. He got to Gillison at the same time as us, and he might get home first.'

'No,' Lynch said decisively, 'we're not giving the Baron any rope, Bill. He may be half-thief and half-detective these days, but if we can get him we've got to. Don't slacken with Mannering. We're not even sure he wasn't party to the *Towers* job, and afterwards double-crossed.'

Bristow shrugged.

'I doubt if he knew a thing about it, and I want to get some results. I know no more about Armstrong's death, or the maid's, than I did when we found the bodies.'

'It'll take time.'

'It's taken too much already. I thought Gillison was our man, but I'm beginning to wonder.'

'You're trying to find a connection between Gillison and Mervin?'

'Of course. But they're shrewd beggars, and it won't be easy. Mannering's not at his flat, nor at the studio.'

'*Isn't* he, by Jove!' Lynch looked thoughtful. 'Then he's hiding out until he can show a presentable face after the gas, Bill. I don't see why you're raising questions, it looks to me a certainty that Mannering was there last night. Have him watched the moment he gets back.

'He'll probably prove he's been to the North Pole,' Bristow grunted. 'Well, what about your end? What's this new company of Mendleson's?'

Lynch pursed his lips.

'I don't know. It seems genuine enough. Fauntley and Sharron are on the board. I don't trust Mendleson far, but this may be one of his genuine jobs.'

'If he has any.'

'As you say. Well, Gillison and his girl are being watched, you'll look out for Mannering and you won't lose Mendleson, by the way, I take it you had no luck at *The Pitcher* last night?'

'I didn't,' Bristow admitted. 'Neither Mannering nor Leverson turned up. But I'll keep tapping the wires, although I fancy they put one across us there.'

'Well, keep at it, Bill. I've a feeling that this isn't going to be one of the unsolved crimes. I—hallo, the old man wants me. I thought he was out.'

Lynch stood up, massive and placid, and went to the Assistant Commissioner's office. Sir David Ffoulkes, gaunt and at first sight forbidding, but at one with his subordinates, was sitting at his desk studying the ceiling with elaborate intensity. Without looking at Lynch he said:

'Is Bristow there?'

'Should be passing—ah.' Lynch reopened the door, to find Bristow coming along the passage. 'Just a moment, Inspector.'

They stood in front of Ffoulkes, enduring one of his many irritating silences, knowing that it promised good news. At last he looked at them.

'Any trace of the Beverley jewels yet, Bristow?'

'Nothing definite, sir.'

'Hmm. Well, some of them have turned up.'

'What!'

'Yes,' nodded Ffoulkes. 'Both Crane and Fauntley have telephoned me. They've each received a postal package, containing their missing stones. Better find out if Sharron and the others have been visited by the same good fairy.' After a short pause he added drily: 'I wonder where the Baron found them?'

CHAPTER EIGHTEEN

REST CURE

'I've *never* been so pleased in my life, it's come just at the right time, when everything looked so black, but I always *did* say you ought to look on the bright side, don't you agree, Lorna?' Lady Fauntley beamed happily about her, while the firelight in that early winter afternoon played on the three women sitting in the lounge of Fauntley's Portland Place house.

Fay said tensely: 'How does this affect Bill?'

'Well, my dear, you can't expect everything at once, but this is a step in the right direction. The police didn't manage to find the jewels but someone did.' She began to pour tea. 'Have you seen John today, Lorna?'

Lorna was looking thoughtfully into the fire.

'No, not yet.'

'Busy on the case I expect,' said Lady Fauntley gently, but with an inflection in her voice that made Lorna look round sharply. Her mother's placid eyes met hers, apparently without guile. 'I wonder if the others were as lucky as Hugo. I expect so. I always expect the best. It makes things so much easier.'

'It makes it damned hard when you're wrong,' said Fay.

'Well, yes, but we have to take that chance, don't we? Clara, for instance, is the last person I would have expected to behave in such a way.'

'What's she been doing?'

'Didn't you know? My dear, it's all over London by now, Rene Crane phoned me only a quarter of an hour ago. It appears that the Baron was at a flat in South Audley Street, and when the police got there poor Clara was unconscious, and the man, Merlin I think his name was, was knocked out. Apparently she and her husband only go about together for appearances. And this Merlin or whatever his name is plays the piano rather wonderfully. Rene says she knows him well.'

'Clara of all people with a lover,' said Fay. 'And the

135

Baron?'

'But of course the Baron got away, he always does, doesn't he?'

Lorna's hands relaxed.

Fay said: 'In a way he's rather wonderful, don't you think?'

'Wonderful?' Lady Fauntley considered. 'Well, clever perhaps, but one can hardly *approve*. I've asked Rene and Mr. Crane to come round for dinner, Lorna. I thought it would be nice. I hope John comes in, if he 'phones up you'll ask him I know, he always makes an evening *go* somehow.'

She broke off as the door opened silently, and Parker's voice came quietly through the firelit room.

'Mr. Mannering, Ma'am.'

'Why *John*!' exclaimed Lady Fauntley. 'I was just talking about you, hoping you would come to dinner tonight. Do sit down. There's plenty of tea and you like it strong, don't you?'

Lorna did not move, while Fay looked up into Mannering's eyes, her own filled with questions. Mannering smiled, and sent a message, unspoken but clear to Lorna. She felt a deep relief after the suspense of the day.

'Any—news?' Fay said.

'Nothing definite I'm afraid,' said Mannering, 'but I've a feeling that we're moving on the right lines.'

'What do you think about it now?'

'I'm more convinced than ever that it was murder,' said Mannering, 'and I think Bristow will be able to prove it before long. What's all this about the jewels?'

Lady Fauntley told him, cheerfully. Mannering assured her that a policeman acquaintance had told him a garbled story that all the *Beverley Towers* gems had been restored, but he had not yet received his own. It was half an hour before he went up to Lorna's sitting-room, and as the door closed behind them Lorna gripped his arm fiercely.

'John, you scared me that time.'

'No need,' he said, his arms tight about her. 'I'm sorry, darling, but I should have let you know. I overslept.'

'You did what?' asked Lorna faintly.

'Overslept, for the second time,' said the Baron ruefully. 'As Mr. Moore. I was home about half-past four, I suppose,

136

and in bed at five. It was turned two before I woke up. Do my eyes look presentable?'

'Yes, why?'

Smiling, he told her of the escapade. She seemed content to sit on the arm of his chair and listen, and when he stopped there was silence for some minutes, the pleasant, companionable silence that had come to mean so much to them both.

'Well,' she said at last, 'you found the jewels?'

'All except the Kransits and the Glorias, but there were other things, Mervin's diary among them,' Mannering answered. 'Cryptic, but I think pretty damning. He was at Beverley for three days—or near enough to have got there quickly.'

'Anything about Bill Armstrong?'

Mannering shook his head.

'So you'll have to go on?'

He nodded. He could have told her that his own life was now in danger. But there was the chance that only Rogerson knew him, and he had no desire to worry her. His own quest for the Glorias had faded into insignificance beside the wider issues.

Lorna said slowly: 'Is Mendleson clear, or any of the others?'

'Mendleson may be, but I'm not sure yet. I sent the jewels back to the two men who are reasonably sound.'

'Do you feel sure about Crane?'

Mannering stirred uneasily.

'I like Theo, and I've know him a long time. It's difficult to believe that he would play any part in it.'

'Yes, I know, but all the members of the gang need not have been a party to the actual murder. Armstrong's at least—if it was murder—was done on impulse.'

'We only think so, it might have been prearranged. And there was no impulse about the murder of the girl Sanders.'

'No. Well, let's go back a bit.' Lorna suggested. '*Are* you sure of Crane?'

'He hasn't been checked up.'

'I thought not. As a matter of fact it wasn't until this afternoon, that I wondered if he was concerned—or both of them, for that matter.'

'Steady!' exclaimed the Baron. 'Let's keep it within bounds.'

'Can we?' Lorna frowned. 'Who would have expected to find Mrs. Mendleson where she was?'

Mannering looked surprised.

'Is that known already? The papers haven't arrived, have they?'

'No.' Lorna was looking at him fixedly. 'It's what made me wonder about the Cranes. You know them well, but we're only casual acquaintances. So why should she ring Mother immediately the papers were out, and start a scandal about Clara Mendleson? If it were just for gossip she'd choose a friend; or you'd think so.'

'But what object could she have had?'

'I don't even know that there was an object, it merely made me thoughtful. And it made me think of something that we both appear to have missed.'

'What was it?' Mannering asked uneasily.

'Well,' Lorna spoke slowly. 'Crane rebuilt the *Towers*, didn't he? He designed all the modernisation, and knew the place inside out. You must see that he—discounting Sharron—had the best opportunity.'

CHAPTER NINETEEN

ACTION FOR SLANDER?

'Everything considered it's the most astonishing business in my experience,' said Theo Crane, his lined face set and serious. Fauntley and Mannering sat opposite to him. 'Jewels like that, returned by ordinary letter post, without any idea who sent them.'

'Only hope the police don't find him,' said Fauntley, more jaunty than he had been for some weeks. 'The only fly in the ointment is that John's haven't arrived. But they may

138

do, they may!'

Crane smiled soberly.

'We can't expect the thief to be too generous, damn it. Well, John, you've got two worries on your mind, I gather.'

'I take it the first has just been mentioned,' said Mannering easily. 'What's the other?'

Crane frowned. Nothing he had done or said suggested that he knew anything about the robbery, although Mannering had slipped in one or two apparently ingenuous questions without result. He was beginning to believe that Lorna had raised an unjustified scare.

'Do you mean you don't know?'

'I can't think of anything alarming, no.'

Crane looked uncertainly from one to the other.

'I hope I'm not dropping a brick. I slipped in to see Mendleson last night, and he was in a pretty bad humour. Sharron had just been, and you were supposed to have warned Sharron and Fauntley off some new company. His solicitor came while I was there. *Did* you warn them off?' Crane asked.

Mannering nodded.

'But Mendleson's as sound as the Bank of England!'

'Is he?' asked Mannering, good-humouredly, but he was trying to see how this development was going to affect him, with his present quest. 'We'll see. Who is his solicitor, do you know?'

'Yes, Hartman. I hope you don't figure in a *cause celèbre*, John, mud has a habit of churning up from unlikely places.'

'Let's try a more cheerful subject,' suggested Mannering.

'Right,' Crane smiled. 'When are you bringing Lorna over for an evening? We're home birds generally you know, and Hampstead's a bit out of bounds, but it's time you came.'

'It's not a month since I spent a weekend with you.'

'It seems longer. I'm thinking of adding to my staff, by the way. We need another man in the house at nights.'

'Ha!' exclaimed Fauntley. 'You keep too much jewellery at *The Laurels* to rely on a safe.'

It was on Mannering's lips to mention Errol, but he thought better of it.

He left Portland Place early, and the only good thing he had discovered was that under the united influence of the Fauntleys, Fay was getting more cheerful.

Mannering was less perturbed by the possibility of facing a legal action than by the fact that it divided his attentions. He wanted to give his whole mind to the problem of the Glorias and the *Towers* burglary, but he could not ignore Mendleson's attitude.

It suggested that the company was genuine. The financier would not dare to face a full inquiry—essential if he brought an action for slander—unless he knew that he could face it with equanimity. Moreover it seemed unlikely that Mendleson would lay himself open to any kind of police investigation if he had been connected with Gillison in the theft of the Kallinovs. Could he be safely ruled out?

His wife presented another problem.

So far Mannering knew definitely of three conspirators—Mervin, Rogerson and Gillison. But none of them had been in a position to get the particulars of the strong-room; there was another operative to find. The list of possibilities had widened, and he went through them in his mind, weighing the pros and cons as detachedly as he could.

They were:

1. Lord Sharron. Known to be jumpy on and immediately before the night of the robbery. Refused to ask for extra help from the police.

2. Reggie Sharron. Kept short of money.

3. Theo Crane. Possessed of a full knowledge of the architecture of the *Towers*. In a position to know the precautions that were taken.

4. Mendleson. Connected with Gillison, queer behaviour on the night of the robbery. Opportunity of examining the strong-room.

5. Clara Mendleson—associated with Mervin, who was clearly involved.

6. Servants. All of good reputation.

His long sleep that morning had its uses, for he was wide awake although it was nearly midnight. He felt the urge to

140

be working, and he telephoned Leverson. For the benefit of those listening on the wire, they chatted for five minutes, and immediately afterwards Mannering went to a call-box. Tanker Tring was back at work, standing near the kiosk. Leverson answered from the other call-box almost at once.

'How's the prisoner?' asked Mannering.

'He's difficult,' said Leverson slowly. 'You won't find it easy to get him to talk.'

'Where is he?'

'In the attic here.'

'You shouldn't have risked that,' said the Baron. 'Bristow's a sight too sharp lately. Can I come over now?'

'Yes, of course,' Leverson assured him, 'but make sure you're alone.'

Mannering hung up, and stepped out of the kiosk. Tring made an attempt to dodge out of sight, and Mannering called out to him:

'A nice night, don't you think?'

'It's perishing cold,' answered Tring sourly.

'With snow in the air,' added the Baron, and as if to emphasise his words the sharp wind whistled along the street, bearing with it the first light flakes of snow. 'What you want is a walk, Tanker, a sharp one across the Park. And instead of walking behind me you may as well keep alongside. I'd enjoy a chat for once.'

'Hmm,' said Tring, dubiously.

'No need to worry,' said Mannering cheerfully. 'All Bristow told you to do was to keep me in sight, he didn't specify whether the view was to be back, front or sideways.'

Tring, out of his depth, fell in beside him. Snow began to fall more heavily, by the time they reached the other side of Piccadilly there was a thin film of white on grass and sidewalk. The Baron reached the gates of the Park, hesitated and turned back.

In a way he hated what he had to do now.

Standing by the kerb as the traffic streamed in both directions, he suddenly moved forward. Moving, he knocked against Tring's legs, and the sergeant fell backwards, while the Baron slipped into the roadway. Traffic swerved and brakes squealed, but he made a passage and as he reached the far kerb a taxi with its flag up slowed down. Mannering leapt for it.

'Aldgate Station, fast!'

He could see Tring, on his feet now and surrounded by half a dozen sympathetic passers-by. The traffic was thick, and Mannering did not think there was any danger of immediate pursuit; nevertheless, reaching the Circus he told the cabby to drive along Regent Street, and then to take side turnings. No cab or car followed them.

'All right,' Mannering said, 'Make for the station.'

Twenty minutes later he was entering Leverson's Wine Street house. Flick opened the door himself.

Rogerson was lying on a small bed in the attic, fully dressed but for his shoes and collar. He glared up as the light flashed on, but his lips were set tightly.

'Still obstinate I'm told,' said Mannering, sitting down on a convenient chair and stretching his legs. 'But not for long, I hope. Rogerson, you've been a damned fool. You tried to murder me, apparently believing I'm the Baron, and I can't blame anyone for wanting to put that gentleman away. I've suffered a lot from him. All the same,' he went on musingly, 'that glass and cabinet remain exactly as they are, and the prints are very clear. Unless you talk there's no alternative but a trip to the police.'

'You daren't do it, they'd want to know why you've waited so long!'

'And who is to say when it happened?' said Mannering airily. 'Do you think the police will believe you if you tell them of your little stay here? I'll deny it, and so will my friend. I've carefully covered the evidence with a large bowl; there'll be no dust on it, so the attempt might have happened half an hour ago.'

Rogerson was sweating.

'Worried?' murmured Mannering. 'You needn't be. The police and I want Mendleson, not you, providing you didn't kill Armstrong or the girl. Tell me all you know about the new company, and you'll be as free as the air. I shall, of course, retain evidence that you were at the Towers during the robbery to make sure you don't let your tongue run away with you, but while you behave you'll have nothing to fear. Why not be sensible?'

'How do I know you're not just talking?'

142

'You don't,' Mannering admitted, 'but you have my word for it.'

Rogerson was breathing fast.

'What figures do you want?'

'Any to implicate Mendleson.' Mannering had pushed the company angle, knowing that Rogerson would say nothing about the jewels, for he was convinced by now that Rogerson had worked with Gillison on them, and that Mendleson was not aware of it. The thing which most worried Rogerson was the robbery—and the murders.

'He keeps them in his safe,' the man said sullenly.

'Where?'

'At South Audley Street.'

'Have you got the keys?'

'No I haven't—but I could get the papers. Let me go and I'll send them to you!'

His breath was rasping now, but Mannering knew he had won: he felt elated, confident.

'I think I'll take a chance on you, Rogerson, but there's a difficulty. Won't he want to know where you've been?'

'No—no. I had arranged to have two days off.'

'Right.' The Baron straightened up. 'I'll have you released in the morning. You'll be followed, and you'll get the papers and post them to me before you go anywhere else. Understand? Remember, those admirable fingerprints——'

Downstairs, Leverson said: 'You're not trusting him, are you?'

'I'm taking a chance because I've got to,' said Mannering. 'If he sends the papers, or copies of them, it might help: but I'm more intent on letting him go than anything else, while having a watertight reason for it.'

'I don't follow you,' Leverson said.

Mannering chuckled.

'It's simple, Flick. Rogerson will contact with Gillison and the others pretty quickly. Can you find me a man to follow him? I want a note of everywhere he goes.'

'Of course—a clever idea.'

'I hope it isn't too clever,' said Mannering, grimly. 'If Rogerson was one of the murderers——'

'What happens if you find proof that he was?'

Mannering looked sombre.

143

'I'd let the police have it.'

'And he'd talk about you.'

'That,' said the Baron, 'would be damned unfortunate, Flick.'

As he walked through the flurrying snow it occurred to him that he could have given Errol the job of watching Rogerson, but he was glad that he had not. Errol might be dependable, but a policeman's respect for the law died slowly, and if Errol made a discovery of importance it was likely to be reported to the police instead of the Baron. Leverson's men were in that respect far more trustworthy.

Whether he was wise in letting Rogerson go, remained to be seen.

Mannering had been away from the flat for an hour, which meant that Tring had ample time to return to it, after reporting the mishap. It was even possible that Bristow would try to construe an assault charge, but Mannering did not think it likely.

Tring was not in the street.

A little worried, Mannering went into his flat. He knew at once that someone was inside.

Sudden alarm, the fear that Bristow was waiting for him, flooded his mind. He steeled himself to show no surprise.

Lorna, muffled in furs, her cheeks glowing with the cold, confronted him.

'Phew!' exclaimed the Baron. 'Am I glad to see you, angel! But have a heart next time and let me know!'

'I couldn't,' explained Lorna. 'I did ring through but you were out. It's lucky I had a key.'

Mannering was eyeing her keenly, sensing that there was something untoward in her visit, that she was labouring under the stress of excitement, for all her coolness.

'Well, what is it?'

'Sharron,' she said.

'What about him?'

'He's tried to commit suicide, at the *Towers*. His wife rang for Fay, who's hurried down there with Mother. I think it's touch and go.'

144

CHAPTER TWENTY

SNOWSTORM

Sharron had taken two hundred aspirin tablets, and his life was in the balance. His wife had found him on his bed, with the empty bottle at his side, and she had summoned the local doctor. A plain-clothes man on duty at the *Towers* had learned what had happened, and informed Horroby immediately. Two doctors were working desperately to save the peer, while downstairs Fay and her mother were sitting, white-faced and tight-lipped: Lorna and Lady Fauntley were with them.

Mannering was with Bristow in the small library.

Outside the wind was howling almost at gale force, and the snow was driving against the windows, its unceasing patter merging with the crackling of the logs in the great open fireplace.

'Why did you have to come?' Bristow eyed Mannering grimly.

'I could hardly stay away,' said Mannering, 'seeing that I'd encouraged his daughter to leave the *Towers*.'

'Hmm. Why did he do it?'

'I'm not clairvoyant, Bill.'

'You know as much as any man,' snapped Bristow. 'Who did you get the Kallinovs from?'

Mannering stared.

'What the devil is in your head now? I haven't seen them since they were here.'

'One day,' said Bristow slowly, 'you'll find it advisable to tell the truth—all of it. But if you won't admit you found the Kallinovs and returned some of them, you can at least tell me why Sharron and Mendleson didn't get their stones.'

'Meaning,' said the Baron, 'that you're linking me with the unknown benefactor? It's a pleasant change, William, but I can't help you.'

'Look here,' said Bristow, 'Sharron wouldn't have tried to kill himself unless he knew something—had been a party to it. If you know he had anything to do with the burglary——'

Mannering stopped him.

'That won't do! You've no reason for connecting Sharron with it, this business might have an entirely different explanation. He's been worried for a long time: as far as I can see, since he first began to consider working with Mendleson.'

'Ye-es.' Bristow lit a cigarette as though to give himself time to think. 'You might say from the time he began to lose money on the Stock Exchange—oh, don't pretend to look surprised. You must have known of that.'

Mannering raised his brows.

'Now we're getting somewhere. You knew Sharron was in need of money, and you've been keeping him up your sleeve for complicity in the burglary? I gave you credit for thinking up something sounder than that. I still think Sharron's chief worry has been the company Mendleson is promoting with him.'

'You do, eh? What do you know about it?'

'Nothing. I know just enough about Mendleson to distrust anything he touches.'

'Who warned you?'

'I'll give you three guesses.'

Bristow shrugged.

'I suppose it was Errol. He shouldn't have talked. For your information, Mannering, we've gone into this new company thoroughly, and we can't find anything wrong with it. It looks as if you've burned your fingers by slandering Mendleson, and it might teach you not to meddle. Sharron wasn't frightened of the company, it must have been——'

'Be wise,' interrupted Mannering, 'and don't commit yourself.'

'Listen to me, Mannering.' Bristow's voice sharpened and Tring, in the shadows, straightened up in his chair. 'There have been two murders, and we're no nearer finding the killer than we were at first. You didn't come down here because you owed it to Fay Sharron. You know something about Sharron's attempt to kill himself. You got the jewels —or some of them—from Mervin's place. Why not admit it?'

146

'Mervin? I—oh, you mean the Baron's last victim? Not being in the Baron's confidence, Bill, I don't know where he found them. I doubt whether he did, it doesn't sound Baronial to me.'

Bristow said sternly: 'Mannering, this is a murder case, you've *got* to tell me what you know.'

'Gladly, Bill, but I don't know as much as you do.'

Bristow stood up abruptly. Tanker Tring rose with him. He had, it transpired, been watching for Mannering's return to Brook Street, but Mannering's rush to the *Towers* and the later developments had robbed his anger at the incident in Piccadilly of its edge.

Horroby of the local police, had been at the *Towers* when Bristow and Mannering had arrived, but he had been summoned to Andover on an urgent case, and was not loath to leave the Beverley affair in the hands of the Yard men.

'This dead girl,' said Mannering unexpectedly. 'You haven't traced the man who was at the dance with her?'

'All I know,' said Bristow, 'is that Mendleson's secretary was friendly with her—he was down here for one day, wasn't he? A man named Rogerson, with a none too savoury past. We are picking him up for questioning, although it might come to nothing.'

Mannering went rigid, fighting against showing his alarm.

If Rogerson was questioned he might break down: if he told the whole story he would implicate Mannering, and the game would be up. A crook's evidence might not be reliable. but a word in court, even vaguely, connecting Mannering with the Baron would start rumour and innuendo that would ruin him in London.

With an effort he stretched his arms and yawned. 'It seems a long shot, Bill. Well, I'm off to bed. I'm tired.'

'You shouldn't work so late,' snapped Bristow.

'I don't work at all,' murmured Mannering. 'I'm one of the idle rich.'

Mannering put a call through to a friend when he reached his room. He had to send a message to Leverson; Rogerson must be kept under cover for a time at least, but it would be dangerous to contact with Leverson direct by

147

telephone.

He discovered from Lorna, ten minutes later, that there had been a full reconciliation between Fay and her mother. Lady Sharron was as shocked by the development as her daughter, but she steadfastly maintained she could offer no explanation.

'Fay's cry is: "Why didn't they tell me he was worried?"' said Lorna, sitting on the end of the Baron's bed while he drank coffee and sat in an easy chair opposite her. About the house the wind was rising in intensity, there was a thick layer of snow on the veranda. He had looked outside, to see the white carpet surrounding them, and he had tried to force back his anxiety.

'I'm more interested in why he was worried,' Mannering said. 'The burglary or the company, and everything considered, I'm afraid it's the burglary.'

'That means he knew Armstrong wasn't in it. It's too beastly.'

'The whole thing is beastly.'

He finished his coffee.

'Of course, Mervin won't stay at the flat for long, and I don't think he'll have much trouble in slipping the police. He'll go either to Gillison's place, or another rendezvous. Rogerson might know where that is, but I can't be sure he'll talk.'

'You've given Theo and the others up?'

'I can't do yet. If Sharron dies we'll be as much in the dark as ever.' He lifted the telephone. There was a pause, and he pumped the rest up and down. 'Hello, Exchange, hello!'

There was no answer.

'I wonder,' said Mannering slowly, 'if Bristow has been playing tricks with this 'phone. Have the others gone to bed?'

Lorna nodded.

'We'll try your phone first,' said Mannering.

They could get no reply, but he was prepared to believe that Bristow had cut the wires leading to Lorna's room as well as his own. He hurried downstairs, with Lorna behind him. In the hall he saw Tring and the plain-clothes man.

'Can I help you, Mr. Mannering?'

'I've put a London call through,' said Mannering, 'but something's wrong with the phone.'

He did not imagine the glint of satisfacton in Tring's eyes as the sergeant grunted:

'There is, sir. The lines are down. We were just in time to get a call through to London an hour ago, but they'll be down now until the snowstorm's over. Twenty-four hours, at least, I'd say.'

Mannering stood rigid, his face expressionless.

It was now nearly five o'clock; by nine Rogerson would be free.

Tring broke in maliciously.

'Anything important, sir?'

'Damned important,' admitted Mannering, covering his anxiety with a sharpness that seemed natural. 'You're sure about this?'

'No doubt about it,' Drew assured him. 'You can see some of the wires down from here.'

Tring turned a chuckle into a cough.

'Have to wait this time, Mr. Mannering, unless you're thinking of driving up. *I* wouldn't like the job, the snow's nearly a foot deep in places.'

Tring was having his innings, and Mannering could hardly blame the man for gloating, but he could not get rid of a heaviness at the pit of his stomach. Like a refrain, a sentence ran through his mind: 'Rogerson mustn't go. Rogerson mustn't go.'

But how to stop him?

He nodded goodnight to the smiling policeman.

Back in his room, he turned resolutely to Lorna.

'Rogerson mustn't go!'

She answered quietly: 'What will you do?'

'I'll have to try and get there.'

'It's almost impossible. They'll be watching the grounds, and they'll follow you. Tring expects you to try, and he'll warn Bristow. He'll have men on your heels all the way.'

Mannering nodded. The emergency had come with a frightening suddenness. Was it possible that the Baron's career would end like this, that he would be forced to drop out of society by the implications at Rogerson's trial?

And Lorna with him?

He stared at her blankly. Unless he could get word to Leverson, he had no chance to avoid a catastrophe. 'I'm coming with you,' Lorna said suddenly.

He stepped towards her, gripping her shoulders tightly.

'Lorna, I'll need word of what's happening here, and I've got to be alone on this jaunt. There's no danger unless I fail to get through, but if I do fail, you'll be implicated. You mustn't chance it, understand?'

Wordlessly she flung her arms round him.

She knew that she might never see him again unless it were furtively; she knew that within twenty-four hours, and even less, the Press might be screeching the story that Mannering was the Baron. The danger was not imaginary, it was real and near them, and the odds seemed hopeless.

He broke away.

'I'll get there,' he said. 'Go downstairs, and try to keep Tring and Drew engaged.'

He watched her disappear, then he slipped into a coat. He thought for a moment of trying to find boots to fit him, instead of shoes, but realised that minutes might make or break his chance.

He turned the light out, and stepped softly on to the veranda. From a room on the ground floor a light was shining through the fast-falling snow. It was difficult to see, and yet the white glare of the countryside was vivid enough. He leaned towards the left, running his hand towards the pillar that had helped him once before. Cautiously he climbed over the balcony rail.

He had to go this way, for the doors would be watched. Tring and Bristow between them would make sure that he did not get away without being followed. They might even try to detain him, and an hour's delay would be fatal.

His hands slipped on the stone, but he found the top of the pillar, gripped it, let himself go.

There was no means of checking or controlling his descent, and it was with a profound sigh of relief that he finally hit the snow.

For a time he lay there, sprawled out and breathless, knowing that the snow's deep drifting had saved him from injury.

He waited for less than twenty seconds, picked himself up, and turned from the house.

In that whirling storm it was impossible to be sure of his direction. He tried to remember the layout of the grounds, but the only thing vivid in his mind were the lines of pine trees. If he could find the avenue he could reach the end of the drive, and once he was on the road it would be easier going.

Easier?

If he made two miles an hour he would do well, and even if he reached the main road—four miles away—by seven o'clock, no traffic would be moving. Through the snow it would be virtually impossible. His only hope was to find a telephone from which he could ring London.

How far did the snow area stretch?

From London it had been negligible as far as Camberley, but Camberley was over twenty miles away. It was more obstinacy than hope that drove him on.

He staggered against a small tree, pulled up by a beam of light, not five yards from him.

He stood quite still, and as he watched he saw the burly figure of a man lurching past him. In the reflected glow of the torch he recognised Tring.

So Lorna had failed, they knew he was out of his room!

Tring blundered past.

To find anyone in the storm was nearly impossible, and the torch did more harm than good. But did Tring know the way to the drive? Mannering hesitated, then followed the sergeant. All the time he could see the dark blur of the policeman's body against the white patch that his torch created in the snow, but there was no sound beyond the flurrying of snowflakes and the occasional whistle of the wind.

The walk seemed interminable as the Baron followed that ghostly light.

The snow was thick but even, walking was difficult but not impossible. Mannering calculated that they had been moving for over ten minutes; they should be near the drive now.

He saw Tring slow down.

Something else loomed out of the darkness.

151

The 'something' grew clearer, and he saw a second man, while faintly he saw the rim of a headlight. His heart leapt as he heard Tring's voice, only just audible although less than ten yards away from him.

'Anyone passed, Edwards?'

'Haven't seen a soul, but it ain't easy.'

'No. Still, keep a close watch. Someone's got away from the house.'

Mannering, listening, rejoiced that his name was not mentioned. Bristow and Tring were keeping that knowledge to themselves; until there was a clear case against him his name would not be generally suspect at the Yard.

'Well, he hasn't passed this way. Sergeant, you haven't got a nip with you, have you? I'm perished in this blasted car.'

'Lucky you don't have to stay in the open,' retorted Tring severely.

There was a pause, as a whisky flask changed hands.

A sudden, desperate hope flashed into Mannering's mind. He could just discern the posts of the gates, which were open, and the headlights of the car were turned towards them. The snow was only inches deep here, and on the road itself there was a chance that the car would run.

He circled round the two men standing by it.

As he drew nearer he could hear their voices again, but he could not see them. Snow had drifted against the doors, but that of the driving-seat opened without trouble, and the effect of the headlights was to put the car itself in darkness.

He slipped in.

If the engine refused to start and the noise gave the others warning he would be no worse off, for they would never find him along the lane; it would merely confirm Tring's knowledge that he was about. But his heart was hammering as he let in the clutch cautiously, and, holding his breath, pulled at the self-starter.

The engine hummed at once.

Three movements as one. Clutch in—brake off—throttle down! The car lurched forward.

He reached the gates and swung left.

The wheels slithered, but he kept on. He had no idea how

close Tring and Edwards were behind him, but he was going too fast for them to hope to catch him up.

And there was no way they could send a call out from the *Towers*.

CHAPTER TWENTY-ONE

MORNING ENCOUNTER

Mannering was on the main road.

Now that the first rush of excitement was over he realised the difficulties and dangers of his manoeuvre, but when they were weighed up he knew that he had done the only thing possible. It was true that he had given Bristow a lever for charging him with taking the car without the owner's consent; but it would only be against Mannering, and it was the worst that could happen provided he reached London, or got the message through.

There were other cars at the *Towers*; Bristow might decide to send men after him but he doubted it. No one at the *Towers* would seriously think he could get far, and Bristow was probably consoling himself with the thought that he was stuck in the lane.

The Baron's lips curved, but there was anxiety as well as triumph in his eyes.

The clock in the dashboard was ticking, and he saw that it was a quarter to six. The speedometer needle was quivering on the twenty-five mark.

Twenty-five miles an hour meant Camberley at seven o'clock, and if the London lines from there were in order he would have ample time. He might even get to Staines before Leverson let Rogerson go, and he could surely get a message from the riverside town.

The suspense was nerve-wracking.

He felt weariness creeping over him insidiously, drugging

153

him, and twice he had to sit up sharply to prevent himself from dozing at the wheel.

Blackwater. Camberley High Street.

It was a quarter to seven; he had made good time, but he wondered whether it was wise to stop and try to find a telephone. The first decision was taken out of his hands, for a milk lorry pulled up in front of him, the brakes squealing noisily. Mannering heard them in time to slow down, but the tyres did not grip firmly, and the Morris slithered helplessly across the road.

Through the steamed up side window he saw the lorry driver walk towards him.

'You all right, sir?'

'Yes, thanks, nothing to worry about.'

'Bloomin' lights.' The man drew a crushed packet of Woodbines out of his pocket and proffered them. 'I'm goin' to have the devil's own job gettin' started again, but now I'm going to 'ave some tea. Sure you'll be all right, sir?'

'Nothing but a scare,' Mannering assured him. 'That tea's a good idea.'

The lights of an all-night café beckoned the lorry driver, but Mannering was more pleased by a kiosk near by.

'I'm going to use the telephone,' he said. 'Order a pot of tea for me, will you?'

The lorry driver nodded as Mannering hurried to the booth. He was wet through, and his feet were icy cold, but he forgot it completely as he took the receiver off the hook.

It was an age before the *brrr-brrr* stopped and he heard Leverson's voice.

'Flick,' said Mannering, and knew Leverson had recognised his voice. 'Don't do anything in the morning, just wait for me.'

'Right,' said Leverson, and there was a tense note in his voice. 'I'm going to ring you on the other line in fifteen minutes. What's your number?'

Mannering gave it, and satisfaction was mingling with uncertainty as he entered the all-night bar. What did Leverson want to say that the police must not overhear?

At a table near a roaring fire sat his lorry driver, in front of two cups of tea, and a plate of meat pies.

154

At the end of fifteen minutes Mannering felt satisfied of body, if less so in mind. Surreptitiously he paid the bill for the two, lifted a hand, and went outside. As he reached the phone-box the bell rang.

His heart was hammering wildly as he opened the door.

'Camberley 13256?'

'Yes.'

'You're through, caller.'

'Hallo, John. Listen, it's important. I've had the Glorias through, from someone who wants to sell in a hurry.'

'Good man. I'll buy them of course.'

'You haven't heard the half,' snapped Leverson. 'Mervin has been arrested, with Clara Mendleson, on a drug charge.'

'You're sure?' Mannering's voice hardened.

'There's no doubt at all. Do you see what it means?'

'They're scared and they've got to sell quickly, yes. Have you any address?'

'No, but I'm meeting my man at Aldgate Pump at ten o'clock. It isn't Smith as he's gone up North, so it's probably Gillison. Can you make it?'

'I'll have a damned good try!'

Mannering rang down, and stepped from the kiosk. As the wind struck against his face, he was too full of the possibilities that this development aroused to ponder over Leverson's insistence that if the Glorias were offered by a 'straight' thief there was to be a straightforward deal. It was typical of Leverson, equally typical of the Baron that he agreed to buy back his own stones. It was part of the game, part of the price to pay.

The burning question was the identity of the man who was offering the Glorias. The Sharrons, Mervin, Rogerson and Smith were out; it must be Gillison or an unknown, and Crane seemed the only other possibility.

He still fought against believing that Theo had played a part in the robbery or the murders, but he remembered his shock when Rene Crane had been playing *Der Jangling und Der Tong*. A small thing, nothing in itself and yet perhaps significant.

As he walked towards his car he saw the lorry driver and a little crowd of people, prominent among them a policeman in blue. Mannering went close by, half-afraid that

155

there might be an inquiry for him. He had taken it for granted that he had no need to worry about pursuit from Beverley, but he might have traded too much on the advantages of the storm. Ebb and flow all the time, not a moment to relax. He reached the crowd.

'You might'—the policeman's voice came clearly—'have caused a serious accident, Larkin.'

'All right, don't keep sayin' it. You've lorst me a job, I 'ope that makes you enjoy yer Christmas dinner!'

'I don't want any lip now.' The law was ponderous.

The lorry driver shrugged and walked across the road to the milk tank. The crowd split up, and the policeman closed his notebook with a snap. The driver's face bore an expression of hopelessness that struck the Baron vividly, and lingered in his mind's eye. He saw him climb into the driving cabin as he reached the Morris.

Mannering hesitated, then hurried back to the phone-box. If there was a chance of pursuit from Beverley it would be as well to know it.

'You won't make it, sir. Trees are down between Hook and Basingstoke, and the road between Basingstoke and Andover is impassable ... about mid-day at the earliest I think, sir. You can get through to Salisbury via Newbury, but it would be heavy going... Very good, sir, thank you.'

It was half-past seven, which gave him ample time to get to Aldgate by ten o'clock. Apart from a suppressed excitement, he felt steady and confident. Things were running as he had prayed they would, he should have no trouble. If necessary he would try to get Rogerson out of the country and pay him well: better that than a talk of Mannering as the Baron.

He was on the other side of Bagshot when he saw the milk-wagon again, and he remembered the driver's hopeless expression after the police interview. He passed it, and then pulled into the side.

The lorry lumbered to a standstill behind him, and Mannering spoke through the open window of the driver's cabin.

'Did I hear you in trouble?'

'Lorst me job,' said the other. 'Perishing perlice! I 'adn't pulled into the kerb, and I was too close ter them lights 'e

156

said. I told 'im I was only on trial, but the swine said I didn't deserve a job, if I couldn't obey the law. Law! If I'd slipped 'im arf a quid——' He broke off, staring at the fiver in Mannering's hand. 'No, reely, sir, you don't need t'do that——'

'Take it, man,' said the Baron sharply. 'Your name's Larkin, didn't I hear?'

'Bert Larkin, sir.'

'If you'll give me your address I might be able to find something for you.'

He scribbled a Fulham address in his notebook, waved, and hurried to his car. Ten minutes had gone, but even had he been more rushed for time he would not have regretted that stop.

He was reminded vividly of Errol, nearly as badly placed as this man would have been. As he drove on, Mannering found himself brooding more over the man Larkin than over the coming climax in the search for the Glorias. Generally speaking the police were trustworthy enough, but here and there would be an exception. A policeman's opportunity for taking bribes or compounding felonies were endless, a constant temptation. The knowledge, for instance, that Tring had of him could easily be turned to account. A fiver, for looking the other way when he was leaving the flat——

Mannering's head jerked up.

The idea that flashed across his mind seemed absurd, but it persisted. If he was right he knew who had killed Armstrong.

There was little sign of the snow in Central London or the City. Slush on the pavements was being rapidly swept away. Mannering was a quarter of an hour early, after stranding the police car and hiring one from a West End Garage. That was now parked in a narrow side street, as he waited near a jeweller's shop window.

The streets were thronged, the traffic nearing its mid-morning peak.

Two or three idlers were about, but no one he recognised. If his belief was justified, he would recognise the man who was to meet Leverson.

157

He saw Leverson walking smartly on the other side of the road, and he reached the Pump exactly on the hour. As he did so one of the loungers moved towards him, and Mannering experienced a surge of disappointment.

It was no one he knew, the theory was blown sky-high. He stood waiting, while Leverson and the other talked. His quarry was a small, undersized specimen with a ginger moustache.

They talked for five minutes, and once a packet changed hands. Leverson nodded at last, and they both turned away. Mannering waited until the little man had started along Fenchurch street, and then followed him, without once looking at Leverson.

The man went to the first bus-stop, took a Number 15, and alighted at Piccadilly Circus. Apparently he had no idea that he was being followed, for he did not turn round once. He went to the Tube. Mannering booked a shilling fare and entered the same carriage as his quarry, but kept at the far end. It was the Hampstead line.

Hampstead——

Mannering refused to listen to the voice prompting him, but when the man got out at Hampstead he felt his heart sinking. The station was near the Heath, and about it the snow was inches deep. Mannering saw his man take the Common road, and he knew it well enough to be sure in what direction he was going.

There was no taxi-rank at the station, but a cab had just deposited a fare. Mannering blessed his luck, and ordered the driver to go to Heathcote Drive.

A hundred yards further along the road they passed the little man, walking fast.

At the corner of Heathcote Drive Mannering climbed out, paid off his cab and waited. A quarter of a mile from the road his quarry came in sight, trudging towards him. Mannering walked along the road, frowning, feeling bitter.

He turned back, and this time passed the little man on the opposite side of the road. At a house called *The Laurels* his quarry turned into a carriage drive, while the Baron forced himself to walk in the other direction, tight-lipped and hard-eyed.

For *The Laurels* was Theo Crane's house.

CHAPTER TWENTY-TWO

LAST EFFORT

From Brook Street Mannering tried to telephone *Beverley Towers*, but most Hampshire lines were still out of order. He called Scotland Yard, and left a message that he would like Inspector Bristow to call him when he returned. He believed he could stall Bristow off long enough to work that night to get at the truth, and his motives were clear-cut.

If Crane was concerned in the actual murder he would do nothing to help him. If his only complicity was with the robbery he would not stand idle.

Leverson assured him that Rogerson was safe. The late editions of the morning papers carried a brief statement that Mervin had been arrested late on the previous night. On being shown that, Rogerson had no longer complained about his prolonged captivity.

Mannering was in bed at half-past twelve, and he slept until half-past five the next morning. No news came through, but another call to the Yard earned the information that Bristow was on his way from Beverley, and was expected at Westminster soon after six o'clock. There was no direct line available to the *Towers*: Lorna had to wait in suspense which would strain her nerves to breaking point. He could do little but he telephoned Parker at Portland Place to keep a call in to the *Towers*, with a message that would be all Lorna needed for reassurance.

He felt no exhilaration; the depression which had settled on him when he had seen his quarry turn into Crane's house increased. Theo Crane of all people! Lorna had seen it first, and had taken the logical view, while he had tried to argue against it because of his personal liking for the man. Even now he hoped he would prove Crane innocent of the murders.

The evening papers carried full stories of the arrest of Clara Mendleson and Mervin. There was a report, too, that Lord Sharron had been poisoned, but the Press carefully

159

avoided suggesting foul play or suicide.

Sharron was still alive.

At half-past six, Bristow rang through. His voice was sharp and hostile.

'Hallo, Mannering, you wanted me?'

'Yes, Bill. I promised you I'd help if I could.'

'Well?' Bristow's interest quickened.

'You'll probably have it yourself by now,' said Mannering. 'Just an association of ideas, Bill, the Mervin-cum-Clara Mendleson angle seemed to be the right one, and I'd heard a rumour that Mervin and Mr. Cornelius Gillison were not strangers.'

'I know that now,' said Bristow crisply. 'I think we've got them. Mervin's admitted being at Beverley on the night of the dance, but he says he did not see the Sanders girl. We may break down his denial, with luck, and we're holding him on the drug charge until we can get something stronger. Mannering'—Bristow's voice grew taut; Mannering half-expected what was coming—'if you know anything else you must pass it on. Two murders, understand that, and the murderers might slip through our fingers through lack of evidence.'

'I can't give you a hint,' said Mannering quietly, 'but I may be able to, tomorrow morning.'

'Oh,' said Bristow.

'For which I hope you won't think it necessary to make a move about the disappearance of a car last night. Do I work on, Bill?'

'I'll ring you in twenty minutes,' promised Bristow curtly.

Mannering had a snack and a shave in the interval.

While he was eating, Bristow walked to the Assistant Commissioner's office. As he expected, Lynch was already there.

Ffoulkes looked up sharply.

'Well, Bristow, what did he want?'

'I think,' said Bristow slowly, 'that he's got something, sir. He wouldn't talk as he did unless he had. He wants until tomorrow morning. He didn't say so, but I take it he wants to have freedom of movement, and—er—he seems worried over an action about the car.'

Ffoulkes' lips twitched.

160

'He needn't be, the last thing I want is the Press to get that story. What do you suggest?'

'That we do what he wants, within reason.'

'Reason being?'

'Well,' said Bristow shrewdly, 'he'll want to move without a shadow, and he may ask us to stop watching Leverson. They're in this business together. If it weren't for the fact that those two lots of jewels had been returned, sir, I wouldn't advise this, but knowing what happened, and knowing Mannering, I think it's justified.'

Lynch brushed cigarette ash from his coat lapel, and Ffoulkes said slowly:

'You can draw your men off Mannering and Leverson for tonight and tomorrow, up till midday, Bristow. If nothing's happened then back they go.'

'Thank you, sir,'

Lynch said uneasily: 'Is it wise, sir? We might catch Mannering making a forced entry, that's almost certainly what he's got in mind. If we do, we'd get his man as well as the Baron. I think it's worth taking the risk. Ease the men off, but have Mannering followed all the same.'

Bristow said with some heat: 'He'd know in a moment if we're playing a double game, and he'd simply sit tight. I know we want the Baron, but the murderers are more important.'

'I think we'll get them through Mervin.'

'We can't prove yet that Mervin was near Beverley on the night of the robbery. There's Rogerson, too, we know he's mixed up with the Gillison bunch and Mannering may have him in mind. We haven't a thing on Gillison yet, either.'

Lynch shrugged.

'Well, I'm opposed to giving Mannering an inch, sir. He *might* be pulling something else off, it isn't beyond him.'

Ffoulkes shrugged.

'It's possible, but I'll take the chance. You can crow if you're right, Lynch. Go ahead, Bristow.'

Soon afterwards Mannering said 'Thanks, Bill' very quietly, and half an hour later he left Brook Street, seeing no sign of a shadow. He reached Fuller Mansions, where he spent an hour carefully assuming the identity of Mr. Moore. Then he phoned Portland Place, to learn that Parker had at last spoken to the *Towers*, and that Lorna was on the way to London. Sharron was still holding on.

At that time Gillison was talking to Mendleson over the telephone, and both men were badly frightened. Gillison's troubles were increased by the fact that Yvonne had secretly left the country on a false passport supplied by her father against emergency. Mendleson was frantic at Rogerson's disappearance, and the knowledge that the police wanted him for questioning.

Leverson had contrived to glean a certain amount of information from Rogerson about one thing.

'I was told that Mannering was the Baron.'

'Who told you? Gillison? Mervin?'

'I'm not talking!'

'How many others believed it?'

'One, as far as I know. You're mighty anxious to find out, aren't you?'

Leverson said suavely: 'Mannering's a friend of mine, and a lie of this kind might do him considerable harm. Why don't you tell the whole story? He's a man of his word and he'll see you through.'

But Leverson was forced to give it up, worried though he was.

He had tried to get in touch with the little man with the ginger moustache, but without success. The little man was worried, too, as he sat in a saloon bar and drank beer in the company of ex-P.C. Knowles—late of *Beverley Towers*—who not long since had learned that Errol had contrived to pick up another job.

Perhaps because of that, Knowles was not talkative.

Midnight struck clearly from a Hampstead church, and the heavy tramp of a policeman's feet faded into silence.

No wind disturbed the keen, cold air, but clouds moved sluggishly across the sky, and there was no moon. In the shrubbery of *The Laurels* the Baron made his way towards the back of the house, cautious and yet unable to avoid crunching the snow.

He had examined the outside carefully, and he admitted that Crane had made a good job of protecting himself against burglary.

162

The Baron had one advantage.

He knew the layout of *The Laurels* as well as that of the Fauntleys' Portland Place home, and he knew where Crane's safe was placed. It was a large one, with room for a man to stand inside, built in the wall of the study and cleverly concealed by oak panelling. Mannering knew the make well, knew also that unless he found the keys he would not be able to open it without dynamite.

He had come prepared for that.

The back of the house was his best means of approach, for it was sheltered by large trees, some in the garden, others on the heath. Nevertheless, the Baron knew that to effect an entry would present him with one of his stiffest problems.

From his waist he uncoiled a stout rope ladder, knotted every twelve inches, one end fitted with a steel hook.

Climbing a pipe close by a window he reached the roof without trouble.

It was fifty feet from the ground, and in the night air it looked twice as far. His glance below was not a nervous one, but cautious—more so because the snow made the slates treacherous.

He crouched for a moment on the sloping roof, then worked his way along it until he was immediately above a window large enough for him to climb through.

The eaves were strong, and would easily bear his weight. He fastened the hook of the ladder into stout oak, then very cautiously he lowered himself, gripping the rope in his right hand.

As he was about to slip down he heard a car engine, and a shaft of light sprang out from the heath road. He flattened against the roof, his heart thumping. The car changed gear as it swung round the corner, and for a matter of seconds *The Laurels* was bathed in a lurid glare.

Then the car went on towards the end of the road, and the Baron began again.

Slowly he lowered himself to the window sill.

The room was the bathroom, and the window was wired for alarm, but he knew exactly where and how it was done, and there was no danger in breaking one of the small leaded panes. That part of the job was similar to the work at Bewlay Mansions, but after he had cracked the rubber handle against the glass he stopped, waiting tensely, half-prepared to hear sounds of alarm. None came, and he picked the pieces of glass out carefully, then slipped the wire-cutters through the hole. By touch he located the wire strung across the top of the window, and snapped it in two.

No alarm, no sound.

He unfastened the catch of the window, and pushed it open. In a moment he was through, but his wet shoes gave a slight squeak as they touched the floor.

He stood rigid. Could that sound escape notice in a house where all the rooms were so close together?

Apparently it had done.

Mannering reached the door, opened it and saw the faint light burning on the landing. To the left were the stairs to the ground floor, to the right the short staircase to the attic rooms, occupied by the servants. Two maids and a cook, Mannering knew, and there was a gardener–chauffeur who slept out.

Crane and his wife shared a room, and unless they had changed it since Mannering's past visit it was the first door on the left past the main stairs. He crept along the carpeted passage, hearing no sound from upstairs or down. First he went downstairs, unlocked and unbolted the front door and left it latched, to make sure of an easy exit.

He was reluctant to gas the Cranes, but dared not take a chance. He wanted the keys of the safe, and he had to treat this burglary with the same impersonal coolness as he had his others. If Crane was implicated in those killings he deserved no mercy.

The door opened to the turn of the handle.

The Baron crept in, and found that the light from a street lamp spread a soft radiance about the room. He heard the heavy beathing of Theo Crane, and a slight stir from Rene. Mannering stood silently by the door, watching carefully, half-afraid of a trap.

There was no further movement.

He drew his gas-pistol from his pocket, and stepped firmly towards the bed, Rene was turned towards the window, her golden hair outspread; she looked very lovely.

Mannering pressed the trigger of his gun. He saw Rene's

lips open a little as the ether began to take effect, and then with a little sigh she settled down into unconsciousness. Mannering turned to Crane——

And he saw the man's eyes flicker open!

It was a moment of acute danger, a moment when the whole attempt could fail. Crane opened his lips, but Mannering's left hand tightened about his throat. There was fear in Crane's eyes as the gas-pistol moved, but he struggled gamely, kicking against the bedclothes. To no purpose, for the gas slowly took effect, and he slumped down.

Mannering put his hand under the pillow, and felt something hard. For a moment he believed he had found the keys, but he drew out an automatic. His eyes narrowed as he tried again, but the keys were not there.

He tried Crane's pockets, the dressing-table and wardrobe shelf, the drawers in two small cabinets; he found nothing. If the keys were in the bedroom Crane had hidden them successfully. Ten minutes passed in futile search, and the Baron hesitated. It was not likely that Crane would tell him where to get the keys, if he let him come round. He knew the man well enough to reckon on a dogged, reckless courage. Rene was not likely to know where they were. He took the chloroform bag out, and pressed the pad against their mouths and nostrils.

He was safe from interference from the Cranes for twenty minutes.

It was difficult for him to understand the bleakness in his mind. He felt none of the usual thrill, no pleasure in what he was doing, had no sense of matching his wits against those of the police, or the occupants of the house. What he was doing was unpleasant to him, and he had to force himself to go on. He left the bedroom and went quietly upstairs to the servants' quarters. He knew that the three slept in one large room, and the door opened easily. He took the key from the inside, closed the door and locked it, slipping the key into his pocket.

Crane's study was a large room on the first floor, and as he expected the door was locked. But it was a comparatively easy task to pick it, using a skeleton key, and he stepped inside within three minutes of reaching it.

Heavy curtains were drawn at the windows.

He closed the door, and switched on a small desk-light.

He knew where the safe was, and yet hesitated. Did he want to prove this business against Crane? Would he derive either pleasure or a sense of justice from it?'

Justice, at all events.

He found the knob which controlled the sliding panels covering the safe, and pressed it. The steel door appeared, but the keys were still missing. A quick search of cabinets and desk did not reveal them. He switched off the light and stepped to the windows. Should he putty them to lessen the risk of an explosion echoing outside?

His eyes glinted suddenly, for beyond the curtains he had glimpsed steel shutters. He pulled them into position.

There were no two minds as to what he should do; he had to blast the safe open.

Next he took strong adhesive plaster from the tool-kit at his waist and ran it round the door, pressing it tightly, aiming to keep as much of the sound as possible confined to the room.

To break open a small carton of dynamite and force it into the lock-hole was the work of a few moments. He followed it with a two inch fuse, and then, taking the curtains down, draped them about the safe to lessen the noise still further. At last he struck a match.

The fuse spluttered as he stepped to a corner of the room, crouching there with his head in his hands. The waiting seemed interminable, but the explosion came at last, a loud *boom!* that shook the floor.

Debris fell about the study, thudding againt floor and walls.

As the last of it fell, Mannering straightened up and hurried to the safe. The door was hanging open, and he could see loosely stacked jewel cases and documents. He drew them out quickly, stuffing the papers into the pocket of his coat. He had to work fast, for the explosion would have aroused the servants; after a few moments of fright they would begin to raise the alarm. Neighbours might be on the *qui vive*, too.

He forced the cases, one after the other.

Three in all; *but the Glorias were not in any of them*!

He stared down at the three sets of jewels, precious

166

seconds ticking by as he overcame the shock of that discovery. He had not dreamed that he would be unsuccessful, he was so certain in his mind that the Glorias would be here that it was like a physical shock.

No sound reached his ears, the maids had not yet started calling.

He needed a breather.

He had looked in every drawer, examined every possible hiding place, but the Glorias were not at *The Laurels*.

Did that mean Crane had them hidden somewhere else?

Mannering kept the papers, but left the jewels in the cases, on the floor, and swung round to the door. It was the work of a moment to strip the plaster away.

He pulled the door open, confused and uncertain in his mind.

And he saw the man standing there, with the gun in his hand.

The shock of the encounter made the Baron stagger, but as he regained his self-control, as he stood staring at the stolid face in front of him, looking into those unwinking eyes, he had another shock: different, almost pleasurable. He knew that he had been right, the theory that had seemed shattered by the visit of the little man to *The Laurels* was the right one. He was looking into the face of Errol, the man who had pleaded so convincingly for work!

And he knew why Errol was here, knew who had named the Baron to Rogerson.

That had puzzled him from the first, he could have sworn no one of the Beverley house party suspected him; but Errol, late of Scotland Yard, could easily have done so.

Had done so, in fact.

While Mannering remembered Crane's smiling: 'I'm thinking of adding to my staff, we need another man in the house at nights.'

CHAPTER TWENTY-THREE

CONFESSION

Before either of them spoke, before Mannering had fully recovered from the shock, the maids began to call out in fright from their locked room. But Mannering was more concerned at the possibility of interference from outside.

He was acutely aware of the odds against him.

Erroll could shoot to kill, with every excuse. Probably he *would* do so, for he would be afraid of the Baron. And when the police came there would be a straight-forward story, the game would be finished for Mannering, dead or alive. Whether Errol had the Glorias downstairs or not he was safe from the police, they would not dream of looking for the stolen jewels there.

So many things needed explanation, although he was sure that he knew the truth.

The shouting and banging upstairs increased.

Errol said in a dangerous voice: 'So I've got you, have I? Where's Rogerson?'

It was the final proof that the Baron needed. Despite the danger he felt an invigorating satisfaction.

'You've got me, have you?' he said. 'What for? Shooting Armstrong when he followed you?'

The gun jerked forward.

'Where's the other stuff?' Errol snapped. 'Tell me that, and I'll let you go, or——'

He was two yards from the Baron, too far off for a sharp attack. The nearness of death or capture was on him, there was no time to bluff, to play with words. A quick dive, safety perhaps but a far greater risk of fatal injury. As he tensed himself for the spring, he did not see the woman approaching. Her sharp words were as much a surprise to the Baron as to Errol.

'Put your hands up!'

The Baron's mind reeled, for that voice was as familiar as his own, although a mask covered her face.

Lorna!

Errol swung round, and as he moved the Baron leapt forward, knocking his gun-arm up. The automatic did not go off, but Errol was fighting like a madman, a fist crashed into the Baron's stomach, making him gasp and stagger back. A foot followed. All thought of Lorna's arrival disappeared, pain and alarm mingled with each other. He did not see Lorna bring the butt of the gun down on Errol's head, nor hear the man's cry as he staggered. He did not feel Lorna's hands on his, hear her urgent words.

'John, hurry! You've *got* to hurry!'

He stood up unsteadily, seeing Errol trying to scramble to his feet. Then very clearly he realised what would happen if the police arrived, and Lorna was caught here. That cleared his head.

'You've got your car?'

'Not mine. I hired one.'

'Outside?'

'Two houses along.'

In Mannering's hand was Errol's gun, and he levelled it towards the ex-policeman, while looking at Lorna.

'Lead the way,' he said. 'Errol, you follow her, I'll be behind with the gun, understand that?'

Lorna was already halfway down the stairs. Errol and Mannering followed her through the front door which Mannering had previously unlatched. As they reached the roadway a policeman ran past them towards *The Laurels*.

Lorna's car was standing in deep shadow, without lights.

She slipped into the driving seat and Mannering forced Errol into the back. A police whistle shrilled out. Lorna let in the clutch, and the car began to move. The shouting and whistling behind them merged with the roaring of the engine as they drove towards the Common.

In five minutes they were safe from pursuit. Mannering turned to Errol, his voice harsh.

'Have you got the Glorias with you?'

'I——'

'*Have you?*'

'Yes, yes! They're here!'

'Keep your hands from your pocket! And listen. I know Mannering, he's told me that Rogerson believed he's the

169

Baron. Rogerson's talked, and says he got that from you. Why?'

'I—I once overheard Bristow saying Mannering was.'

'And you believed it? It takes an ex-policeman to do that! According to Rogerson he and Smith were getting away with the stuff when Armstrong came out. You shot him. They planted the suitcase with the big stuff in the shrubbery, came back and chucked Armstrong into the hollow, after planting the small jewels on him. Right?'

'Y-yes.' Errol was shivering.

'Afterwards you heard the maid talking to young Sharron. You found she suspected you. Rogerson and Mervin came down the day Sharron kicked you out, went to the dance with her, and afterwards walked to the stream. You pushed her in——'

'It's a lie!' Errol screeched. 'Rogerson did it, I couldn't stop him, Mervin held me up with a gun! Where is Rogerson.'

'He's well looked after. Who else did you tell about Mannering?'

'No one, I swear! Gillison wanted to know, but I wouldn't talk.'

'Meaning that you saw a chance of blackmail and you were afraid Gillison would steal your thunder?'

'I—oh, for God's sake, yes, yes!'

'How did Rogerson get the idea?'

'I—I told him, I had to! Gillison sent me to find if Mannering knew about—about his part. When I saw he did, Gillison told me to croak him. I daren't, I told Rogerson and he went to Brook Street.'

'So you're the only two who think it,' said the Baron. 'Look!' He switched on the roof-light, and took off his mask. Errol stared into that unfamiliar face. 'Satisfied?'

'Y-yes, *yes*!'

'You'd better be. Now you're going to turn King's evidence,' went on the Baron very slowly. 'Understand? It's your only way of saving your life. You'll testify against Gillison, Mervin, Smith and Rogerson.'

'I—I *daren't*!'

'Here's the alternative,' said the Baron, and he raised his gun. Errol crouched back in the car.

170

'All—right.'

'Sensible man. Was Yvonne Gillison in this?'

'No.'

'Mrs. Mendleson?'

'No. Mervin got friendly with her in order to find out Mendleson's game, but—but she didn't know it.'

'I see,' said Mannering, and then very softly: 'What *is* Mendleson's game?'

'I don't know, I swear I don't.'

'All right. Why did you type that letter to Mannering?'

'It—it was Gillison's idea,' Errol muttered. 'He told me to send it, but he didn't tell Smith or Rogerson about the Baron being there, when Armstrong butted in it looked easy to them to plant the stuff on him. I—I was too busy watching the house, I didn't know what they were doing.'

'That was unfortunate,' murmured the Baron. 'When Mannering arrived outside, Smith or Rogerson knocked you out, to prevent you from being suspect. One thing and the other must have made Gillison see red.'

'He nearly went mad,' muttered Errol.

But for the nagging fear that Rogerson would name him in Court, Mannering was well satisfied. He learned that Errol had been planning a scheme of blackmail, but had hesitated. Needing money badly, Errol had joined Gillison, and hearing of the plot to get the Kallinovs, had boasted of his knowledge that the Baron would be among the guests. Gillison had worked on that to implicate the Baron and gain time for getting the stones out of the country, but he was handicapped by Errol's stubborn refusal to name the Baron.

Mannering could safely put Bristow on to Gillison, now.

To save himself from possible trouble it would be easier to let Errol and Rogerson go, even to help them abroad: but to condone murder was beyond him, he had to take the chance.

He asked Lorna to pull up at the nearest phone kiosk.

'How the devil did you do it, darling?' he whispered.

Her smile was quick, anxious.

'As soon as Parker phoned I came down—you were leaving Fuller Mansions as I arrived, and I knew you were after the Cranes when you booked for Hampstead. So I hired the car.'

'Bless you,' said the Baron fervently. He turned back to Errol, and spoke more loudly. 'How did you get the job with Crane? You were working there, weren't you?'

'I—I pitched the same yarn as I did to Mannering, and his wife was nervous after the *Towers* job, and he took me on.'

'Who's the little man who saw Leverson?'

'He's Gibson—he runs messages, he don't know much.'

'Was Knowles in it?'

'No—he knows Gibson, that's all.'

Lorna pulled up by a kiosk, and Mannering slipped out, leaving her with a gun to control Errol. He was through to the Yard quickly, and in a few seconds Bristow's voice came over the wires.

'Yes, Mannering?'

'Up late?' asked the Baron. 'Gillison is your man, Bill, and Errol's another. Errol will give you your evidence, for the usual clemency, and he's got the Glorias in his pocket.'

'You *sure*?' gasped Bristow.

'Not a doubt. But I can't hand you Mendleson on a salver, more's the pity.'

'You don't need to,' Bristow said. 'Sharron recovered enough to talk. The whole company was to be "genuine" until it was floated—they had rented a factory, even taken orders for goods. But they were going to decamp afterwards —or Mendleson was. He's deep in a dozen frauds, and he had to get out of the country. He needed Sharron's name on the board to get hold of others: Sharron wanted money quickly, and fell for the bait. He was to have a third of the proceeds, and Mendleson was to disappear with the rest, taking the blame. When you warned Sharron about Mendleson he cracked.'

'But Fauntley——'

'Oh, he wasn't in it, he simply persuaded Government orders for the new company. We've taken Mendleson, and I'll get Gillison before the night's out. Sharron died soon after signing a statement.'

'It's as well,' said Mannering slowly.

It was over. Mendleson's ramp as well as Gillison's, two

172

major crimes apparently unconnected—and he could return the Sharron jewels, and the Mendleson's, to the proper quarters.

But would Rogerson face trial without trying to implicate him?

It was more likely that the man would try to win sympathy from the police by naming the Baron, and a word in Court would break Mannering, even if there was no reliable evidence.

Breaking the Gillison gang might bring his own downfall.

Rogerson's face was livid as he stared at the Baron.

'You daren't do it! I'll let the world know you're the Baron!' He sobbed for breath, his body quivering. 'You promised me a break——'

'That was before I knew who killed Armstrong,' said the Baron sombrely.

'It will ruin you!'

'You can't name me,' said the Baron slowly.

But he knew that if Rogerson persisted it would break him, and there was no reason for the man to keep silent: his one faint hope of avoiding the gallows was a reprieve in exchange for information.

Rogerson's eyes were glassy, and his voice dropped.

'You—you mean it,' he gasped. 'No, I won't face the police. I didn't mean to kill, I swear, I didn't.'

His hand moved like lightning from his pocket to his mouth, and a moment later Mannering and Leverson caught the sharp smell of bitter almonds. They had to watch him die.

Bristow glanced with satisfaction at Superintendent Lynch.

'Errol's story fixes Gillison, Smith and Mervin, sir. Rogerson, too, but he's been found dead on Wanstead flats —prussic acid, obviously suicide after he heard about the arrests. Smith has been picked up in Manchester, and he confirms all Errol says.'

'Good. Anything else, Bristow?'

'From papers at Mendleson's place, sir, it's pretty obvious he and Gillison were planning the separate coups together, and to leave the country. I fancy Mendleson would have bought the Kallinovs, but he hesitated when the Baron raided the Barnes house, and Gillison wanted to sell quickly. There's another odd thing'—Bristow's lips twitched—'Errol's anxious to help us now, and he's convinced we're wrong in thinking Mannering is the Baron. I fancy he's sincere, but I heard something rather unexpected —you know Errol's wife has T.B.?'

Ffoulkes raised his eyebrows.

'What about it?'

'Mannering's arranged for her to go to Switzerland, where she's got a good chance of pulling through. That's one of the reasons Errol went into the game, apparently. Anyhow, he's cock-a-hoop over it, and strong for Mannering.'

'Since Sharron died, it's fairly satisfactory all round,' admitted Ffoulkes. 'A very successful inquiry, Bristow. Your arrest of Errol earned a lot of publicity. So has the Baron since he returned the Sharron jewels to Lady Sharron, and Mendleson's to the Public Prosecutor. I want you to take an hour or so off this afternoon.'

'Do you, sir?'

'Go and have tea with Mannering,' said Ffoulkes, taking a string of diamonds from his desk, 'and return the Glorias with our compliments.'

THE END